# Rambler

## Books by the Author

LESLIE & BELINDA MYSTERIES
*Daredevil*
*Shanghaied*
*Rambler*
Coming August 2017
*The World's Longest Yard Sale - is Murder*

*Pickett House: Tennesee Haunting Fiction*

PARLOR GAME MYSTERIES
*Hanging Tobacco*

# Rambler

## A LESLIE & BELINDA MYSTERY

by

## Linda S. Browning

Buddhapuss Ink • Edison NJ

Cover Art background based on a design by Svetlanaprikhnenko,
Dreamstime.com
Cover and Book Layout/Design by The Book Team
Editor, MaryChris Bradley
Copyeditor, Andrea H. Curley
ISBN 978-1-941523-15-5 (Paperback Original)
First Paperback Edition July 2017

PUBLISHER'S NOTE

The Buddhapuss Ink LLC name and logos are trademarks of
Buddhapuss Ink LLC. www.buddhapussink.com

Learn more or contact the author at:

Facebook: LindaSBrowningAuthor
Twitter: @LindaSBrowning
Website: lindabrowning.net

# DEDICATION

My LESLIE & BELINDA MYSTERIES will forever be dedicated to my best friend since the summer before we entered the eighth grade. Lynne, these are for you.

Thanks to all the oddball people who have inhabited my life thus far: family, friends, neighbors, enemies, et al. Some are no longer with us, but their eccentricities live on.

# Chapter One

ram·bler \ ˈram-blar \ **noun** : a person who goes on long walks for pleasure; a plant that grows up and over fences, walls, etc.

**Synonyms** : Drifter, gadabout, gypsy, knockabout, maunderer, roamer, rover, stroller, vagabond, wanderer, wayfarer.

*~ Merriam-Webster*

**The Nash Rambler**: a North American automobile that was produced by the Nash Motors division of Nash-Kelvinator Corporation. From 1950 to 1954. The Nash Rambler established a new segment in the automobile market and is widely acknowledged to be the first successful modern American compact car.

*~ Wikipedia*

I abhor shopping. Allegedly girls prefer shopping over almost any other activity. This was never the case with me. No longer a girl, I am sixty-nine years old. I experienced no life-shattering alterations as I advanced from sixty-eight to sixty-nine. My body didn't begin to convulse at the stroke of midnight or anything. I know because I was prepared for it.

When I was a teenager, the number sixty-nine was infamous. The alphabetic spelling of the number had no significance other than representing the number following sixty-eight. The numerical version became a secret code for an agile sexual maneuver. At the time, a lot of us didn't appreciate what was so scandalously naughty about 69. That didn't stop us from scrawling it all over our lockers and decorating sidewalks with chalked 69's while giggling like fools. I was probably seventeen when I learned that 69 had something to do with sex of an orally reciprocal nature. I grew up when girls were not as knowledgeable about sex as they are nowadays. Even when I finally grasped the meaning behind the whole 69 phenomena, it impressed me as a rather dyslexic gymnastic maneuver.

But I digress. The topic was shopping: I would rather have a root canal than go shopping just for the sake of shopping. At least a root canal comes with the benefit of anesthesia. Oh, I enjoy noodling around in the Dollar General Store here in Fairlawn Glen and at the Big Lots in the nearby town of Clifton, Tennessee, but big-time shop-till-you-drop stuff? Nope, not me, count me out; perhaps it's a hormone deficiency.

In late March, two months into my scandalous age, I finally gave in and accompanied my best friend, Belinda Honeycutt, on a shopping excursion to the Turkey Creek Mall outside of Knoxville. Belinda and I are both widows and reside in the Lake Manchester Townhomes in Fairlawn Glen, a retirement/resort community located in Middle Tennessee. I live in Unit 2 with my dog, Riff-Raff; and Belinda lives in Unit 5 with her cat, Butter. My husband, Tom, dropped dead of a heart attack on the thirteenth hole at the golf course six years ago. Belinda's husband, Frank, eventually managed to pickle his liver in alcohol almost three years ago.

Belinda still drives the 1998 Buick Riviera that Frank bought for her when he heard the model was being discontinued. I can see why. It's a monster with a long, sleek, low-slung body. Crawling in and out of it reminds me of playing Twister back in the sixties. The heavy door snaps shut behind me like a Venus fly trap. I've never driven Belinda's car, until today that is. If not for a medical emergency during the shopping excursion—which I didn't want to go on in the first place—I would've never attempted to motor around in that behemoth.

One hour into the shopping adventure I was already bored with the meandering nonsense required of stereotypical lady-shopping. I was sitting by a fountain waiting for Belinda to come out of the Victoria's Secret store when a saleslady came hustling out and made a beeline for my fountain. She came right up to me and asked me if I was Leslie Barrett. I said I was because, well, I am. It wasn't a big challenge picking me out of the lineup since the choice was one of the five men sitting around the fountain waiting for women or me.

Belinda had toppled over in the dressing room struggling with some kind of Wonderbra contraption. Seriously, the scandalous 69 maneuver doesn't have anything on the contortions required to fasten one of those boob lifters. Belinda had been flailing her almost six-foot frame around in a dinky dressing room in an attempt to secure the bra closure when she collided with a hanger, knocking it to the floor. Caroming about the closet-sized dressing room, she stepped on the hanger, turning it into a roller skate, and ended up in a tangle of arms and legs on the floor. Sufficiently discombobulated and hopelessly entangled with pain shooting through her right shoulder and foot, she howled for a saleslady to round me up at the fountain. Belinda was a nurse. I was a geriatric social worker, but I didn't have to be a nurse to recognize when a soon-to-be seventy-one-year-old woman has sustained significant boo-boos to her right foot and shoulder. Wondering if her shoulder was merely dislocated, I suggested she try slamming herself against the wall of the dressing room to reset the shoulder. I had seen Mel Gibson do this once in a movie. Belinda's glare in response to my helpful suggestion could have frozen dirt. I'm only five-two and stood on the cut out shelf area intended for sitting as I maneuvered around her tall frame squished into the dressing room. What a rodeo! I couldn't stop giggling.

"Leslie, this isn't funny. I'm in pain!" Belinda ground her teeth.

"Ha-ha-ha, I know, Belinda, I'm sorry. Ha-ha-ha." I prayed there were no hidden cameras; then again, if there were cameras, I definitely wanted to burn those pictures to a disk. Once she was presentable, she tried to put weight on her foot, but she was obviously in distress. I took charge.

I backed her up to the sit-shelf thing, and she plopped down. "Sit here, Belinda. I'll get a wheelchair."

"I. Don't. Need. A wheelchair," she growled.

"Hey, I didn't even want to come to this stupid mall, so don't growl at me. I had to leave my dog home and everything. What would you suggest we do? You obviously cannot walk. I obviously cannot carry you. Unless you want to crawl, the logical solution is a wheelchair." This is what social workers do, you see: we take charge of emotionally stressful situations. If blood and/or vomit are present, I could qualify as an Olympic runner-away. Give me a nice, clean emotional crisis, and I shine.

The salesladies were very helpful, and pretty soon one of them came wheeling a chair through the store. She helped me transfer Belinda from her slumped position on the sit-shelf thing into the wheelchair. I had worked in a nursing home but never developed the knack for driving people around in wheelchairs. I was always pushing a chair without releasing the lock or banging the patient's foot lifting and/or lowering the stupid pedal-like footrest things. After a while nobody would let me help anyone in a wheelchair—fine by me. Still, my friend needed me. I went huffing behind the chair and managed to navigate through the shop without doing any further damage to either it or my friend. I was doing well until we got to a few steps with a ramp beside them. Belinda went rolling down the ramp practically dragging me behind the chair. It reminded me of my youth when I used to roller skate. I was pretty good until I had to stop.

We managed okay, and Belinda even chuckled through the pain a couple of times. One of the security guys helped us maneuver the parking lot to the Riviera. That was when the real challenge presented itself. Approaching the car, Belinda spoke up and over her shoulder, "You're going to have to drive, Leslie."

My step stuttered and, speaking to the security guard, I instructed, "Call for an ambulance. There is no way I can pilot that big boat out of here."

"No, no, no," Belinda objected, "I am not going home in an ambulance. You are perfectly capable of driving back to the Glen."

"Maybe you need X-rays," I suggested hopefully.

"Nice try. You can do this. That car practically drives itself."

"Good." Turning to face the Buick I ordered, "Riviera, take Belinda home." Security guy laughed.

The security guy had scrounged up a couple of ice packs. We reclined the passenger seat until Belinda's head was practically lying on the backseat. Her foot was beginning to swell. I gently removed her shoe; she cursed the entire time. We elevated her foot with our purses and put one bag of ice on her foot and the other wedged between her sore shoulder and the door. She would have been more comfortable in the backseat; but the stupid Riviera is a luxury sports car, and evidently there is some kind of car rule that a sports car cannot have more than two doors, which is just stupid. This car was clearly intended for Gumby-people.

Reluctantly I got behind the wheel. Belinda talked me through how to zoom the seat up far enough to reach the pedals and the steering wheel. "So, great," I grumbled, "now if I could just see through the stupid windshield, we might actually be able to go somewhere." There was another lever she told me to monkey with that raised the seat up. Once I was all zoomed in and perched up, I asked, "Now what?"

"Buckle up and turn on the ignition, Les. You'll be fine."

I took a deep breath and did as my best friend in the whole world instructed.

The Buick has a long nose, and trying to gauge your proximity to objects is impossible. "These mirrors must have been installed at a fun house. I can't tell where the car leaves off and the rest of the world starts. I have zero perspective," I groused.

"You're just short. There's nothing wrong with the mirrors." Then she groaned loud and long. I decided to keep any further complaints to myself for the time being. It took several minutes of jockeying between Drive and Reverse to back out of the parking space. My patient emitted little wincing squeaks every time I shifted gears. It was hard to tell whether she was in pain or in mortal fear for her beloved Riviera—probably both.

Once I was in the going-forward mode of travel, I crept from the mall lot and onto the residential street. The mall is situated close to the entrance to I-40, but I still had to drive a few city blocks to get to it. A horn honked behind me. "Les, speed up a little. You're driving like a little old lady."

A car whooshed past on the left, and I got a glimpse of laughing young faces. "Did you see that? That guy passed us. This is a two-lane street with no passing." I threw my hand toward the middle of the road. "See there, a solid-yellow line. No passing!"

My friend mumbled, "Little old lady."

We went another city block, and the street expanded to four lanes. I stopped at the already-red light and glanced to my left. "Look! It's those kids again." I got an idea. "Hey, the Riviera is supposed to be a sports car, right?"

"All I know is, Frank said the engine is a supercharged V-six. In Frank's words, 'That sucker can fly.'"

The light changed to green, and I stomped my size 5½ red Keds tennis shoe on the accelerator. I peeled away from the traffic light with squealing, smoking tires, leaving the laughing young people in the dust. I yelled, "*Whoo-hoo!*" Grinning, I crowed, "Little old lady, my butt! I'm the little old lady from Pasadena! I started singing, "Go Granny, go Granny, go Granny go!"

Belinda groaned, "Oh my God, I've created a monster."

# Chapter Two

The Buick really flew down the expressway. I was reminded of Barbara Eden in one of the earliest episodes of *I Dream of Jeannie*. It was as smooth as a magic carpet ride. I looked at the speedometer and realized I was going eighty-five. Belinda had to talk me through setting the cruise control so we wouldn't get pulled over by the police.

I was enjoying myself until we got closer to Clifton. Belinda's foot was swelling rather spectacularly. She wanted to go home, but I was afraid that once we got home, I wouldn't be able to get her back into a car again. Against her protests, I drove to the Clifton, TN, regional hospital.

Upon arrival at the hospital emergency room, I pulled up to the entrance and ran inside for a wheelchair and some muscle. I then informed everybody that it was physically impossible for me to park the Riviera. So unless the hospital people wanted the car to sit out front until my friend was patched up and ready to go, somebody else would have to do the parking, and later on the getting. Fortunately, folks in the South are eager to help. I am originally from Flint, Michigan, and Belinda is from Philadelphia. Ask for assistance in the northern states and hell will literally freeze over because, well, everything eventually freezes over in the North.

The intake lady at the ER desk wore a name badge: BECKY PHILLIPS. Becky asked how Belinda had injured her foot. My friend gave me a look of desperation that pleaded, "Do not tell these people I tangled with a push-up bra at Victoria's Secret."

I blurted, "We went shopping at the Turkey Creek Mall. Belinda stepped on a piece of gum in the parking lot and started hopping back toward the car with her gummy shoe in one hand. She lost her balance, and her shoeless foot landed on one of those concrete bumper things that they use in parking lots. She fell on the arch of her foot pretty hard." I came up with this story so quickly because the exact same thing had happened to me in August at the Clifton Outlet Mall, except I didn't break my foot. Of course, Belinda had been with me that day, so she was familiar with the story.

"That's right." She nodded vigorously.

"How did you injure your shoulder?" Intake Becky asked.

Belinda sent me another helpless look, so I jumped in to embellish the lie. "She fell into her Riviera. Have you ever seen a 1998 Buick Riviera?" I rolled my eyes. "That car is a beast, an absolute beast! Belinda caromed off that sucker and sat right down in the parking lot. I wouldn't be surprised if she sues those Turkey Creek Mall people."

Wrinkles appeared above Intake Becky's eyes. "Why would she want to do that?"

I puffed up in righteous anger. "They have a responsibility to keep their parking lots safe for customers!"

Becky looked incredulous and shook her head. "But how could it possibly be the fault of Mall Security that your friend stepped on a piece of gum and then fell onto her own car?"

I waved my arms expansively. "How should I know? I'm sure there are parking lot rules and regulations to cover this sort of thing. There must be inspectors or something."

"What are they supposed to inspect?" Poor Becky was genuinely trying to follow my line of reasoning.

Belinda cut in irritably. "I'm not going to sue anyone. I *am* going to

start hollering pretty soon if somebody doesn't get me some pain med-
ication and some X-rays, and in that order!"

The X-rays revealed a metatarsal stress fracture in her right foot, and
she was fitted with one of those inflatable walking boots. Her shoulder
was only bruised, so it was a good thing she had nixed Mel Gibson's
miraculous shoulder cure.

The hospital people didn't ask any more questions about the accident.
I told everybody who would listen how I had heroically driven the
1998 Buick Riviera all the way back to Clifton from Knoxville by my
little ole self.

Once Belinda was as patched up as she was going to be, somebody
fetched the Riviera and had it idling at the sliding entry doors. I went
around to the driver's side and settled in behind the wheel to watch
as a nurse and an orderly loaded Belinda into the passenger seat while
being careful not to jostle her booted foot more than necessary. I waved
farewell to the hospital people.

Once again in the going-forward mode of travel, I drove us back
to Belinda's place by my little ole self and parked the monster in the
driveway. I refused even to consider maneuvering that tank into the
garage. I couldn't tell how far I was from the garage door, so I hefted
the heavy car door open and bobbed in and out of the car, creeping up
on the door by inches.

Belinda finally snorted "Oh for pity's sake, just leave it."

"Gladly." I huffed, slammed the door, and circled the massive vehicle
to assist my banged-up friend. Once she was finally vertical and leaning
heavily on me, she hop-hobbled in through the front door. I parked
her on the sofa with her foot propped up on an ottoman, hunted down
Butter, and plunked the growling cat next to her. I covered them both
with a blanket, fed Belinda a couple of pain pills, and left to pick up
my dog from Mrs. Towers.

My dog, Riff-Raff, is an eight-pound Maltese/something-else dog of the female gender. When she hit the ten-pound mark, Riff went on a diet. I usually take her everywhere, but the Turkey Creek Mall people are a bunch of snobs, so I had left her with Mrs. Towers. Mrs. Towers is an eightyfive plus-year-old widow friend of ours who resides in Unit 19 of our complex. She is going on her third year of being eighty-five. She gets around pretty well with a walker for eighty-five-plus. She has one of those *help-I've-fallen* gizmos, but it never seems to be anywhere nearby when she falls. Fortunately, she has wall-to-wall carpeting, as I do. I do not understand why older people elect to reside in single-level homes to avoid stairs and then put in hardwood flooring. Carpeting cushions a fall whereas hardwood is a blunt instrument to the back of the head. Quality carpeting is also kinder on the arthritic knees of an older person. I float to the floor with the grace of a balletic fairy. I rise with grunts. When I find myself nowhere near anything substantial enough on which to lever, I am reduced to log rolling across the carpeting until I encounter something. Riff likes it when I log roll. She thinks it's a grand game.

Mrs. Towers knows everything that goes on in Fairlawn Glen and passes along her information to us. She drives into Clifton three times a week, to Lilly's Beauty Shop to get her hair done and to fine-tune her gossip channel. She really shouldn't be driving. She goes twenty-five miles an hour regardless of the posted speed limit. I never thought I'd see the day when her mind would wander off without her; lately, she has been coloring outside the lines a bit. It made me nervous leaving my little mutt with her.

At the end of the day, I have to admit: I don't hate that big-@$$ Buick Riviera as much as I used to. Once in the going-forward mode of travel, that car is a sweet ride. I still hate shopping.

# Chapter Three

Belinda was stuck wearing what they call a tall pneumatic walking boot. It looks like something out of the movie *RoboCop*. It has bladder pumps that inflate and deflate for stability and comfort, an oxymoron if I ever heard one. I understand that a car's air bag inflates as a matter of personal safety, but I wouldn't want to spend a significant amount of time crammed up next to one. I can empathize with Belinda's plight because I had corrective surgery on both feet when I was in my forties. I had to stomp around in Frankenstein boots for weeks—awkward, pain-filled stomps. I didn't have fancy balloon boots. I believe I was legally insane before the rehabilitation period was over. Later on, the same orthopedic surgeon wanted to *fix* my crooked little toe. I told him in colorful language what I would do to him if he came anywhere near my little toe.

Belinda's been in that boot for two weeks and has at least two more to go. She can't drive, so I chauffeur her to and from doctor's appointments and stuff.

Normally I attend the Catholic church; I became a Catholic upon marriage. Previous to Tom, I had been a Methodist. Since Belinda is Methodist, and I am familiar with the Methodist routine, I've been substituting Methodist services for Catholic mass. My local priest gave me some grief about it, but I told him I was only taking a hiatus from mass to accommodate my friend during her recovery period. He was quick to point out that they have Catholic mass practically on the half hour to accommodate busy people. Despite my priest's lamentations, I'm not worried. God knows where to find me. I'm pretty sure the Methodist and the Catholic prayer channels are tuned to the same frequency. I have no intention of running from church to church every Sunday just to put in an appearance. Religion shouldn't be a scavenger hunt. Variety is the spice of life.

Mrs. Towers also attends the Methodist church, so my white Kia Soul has become a mini church bus. I was enjoying fraternizing with a congregation other than my own. I liked the prayer card segment of the Methodist service. Each Sunday members of the church filled out individual prayer cards asking people to pray for so-and-so who was having another surgery on the same knee or having surgery on the other knee or was recuperating from surgery on one or both knees. Methodists have bad knees. They wouldn't last ten minutes as Catholics. The minister reads out the cards to pray for so-and-so for whatever reason, and little gasps of "Oh my" or "Oh dear" or "Oh no" flitter across the congregation. To me, it was religiously sanctioned gossip. The first two Sundays I slipped in a card for Eric. Eric's uncle, Roy Conklin, is a fellow Methodist churchgoer. Poor Eric got himself lost months ago in the wilds of Idaho trying to prove that he was a trained survivalist. Clearly, Eric didn't graduate anywhere close to the head of that class, because he hasn't been heard from since he went solo trekking without a cell phone, compass, flashlight, or book of matches.

It took Belinda and Mrs. Towers two weeks to catch on, and they forced me to stop. The first card said, "Pray for Roy's nephew, who is out there somewhere." I got that line from the mouse movie when the two mice siblings are singing to each other across the miles. I like that mouse movie, and the song. The second card said, "Pray that no one from the search party goes missing while looking for Roy's wilderness-trained nephew, Eric." For some reason Belinda and Mrs. Towers fussed at me about the prayer cards. Sheesh, I try to be sensitive, and all I get is grief.

The tulip fiasco was a fun Sunday though. Tulip Sunday is a yearly event to kick off spring. The Women's Church Group offers pots of tulips that can be purchased before the service to be planted in memory of a loved one. I admit that the sanctuary was beautiful, with hundreds of pots of tulips stacked here and there for the congregation's viewing pleasure. Just before the service concluded, a representative from the Women's Church Group announced that there were some extra pots of tulips. If anyone wanted them, they should see her immediately after the recessional.

Now, I have no idea what those people *thought* she said, but it sure wasn't what she'd meant. Before the organ music faded, women swarmed in a tulip-feeding frenzy. The happy, flower-fueled crowd trampled the tulips, leaving forlorn petals, clumps of dirt, and colorful strips of cellophane in its wake. It looked like cleanup at Walmart the morning of Black Friday. Belinda and Mrs. Towers stood looking down at the dirt and cellophane strewn about, shaking their heads in bewilderment. "I realize I'm new around here, ladies, but I get the feeling this didn't go as planned."

# Chapter Four

It was early April, and we were going looney with boredom. Just when we'd turned the corner from winter to spring, Belinda goes out and gets herself packed into a balloon boot. Feet hurt a lot, even when they're *not* broken. Belinda was in considerable pain the first time I drove her to the doctor's office for her follow-up appointment. We were relieved when we finally made it to the waiting room, to wait and wait. Finally, a lady called out, "Belinda Honeycutt." I was irritated because I don't wait well. Belinda was miserable because her foot was (as my mother used to say) throbbing. I followed Belinda's rocking gait to the counter to await further instructions.

"Mrs. Honeycutt, please proceed to exam room ten. The doctor will be with you shortly," a lady said, staring at her clipboard.

I couldn't believe what I had heard. "Excuse me, miss, did you say room *ten*? Exam room ten is at the *end* of this hallway."

"Yes, ma'am, the doctor will be with you shortly," she repeated, never looking up from her clipboard.

Belinda tried to head me off, but it was no use. "Miss, I'd like to point something out to you." I tapped her shoulder until she acknowledged me. Leaning in close to the young woman, I spoke slowly. "For future reference, put the broken hands and fingers in exam room *ten*. The broken feet and legs should be put in exam room *one or two*." By the time I had completed my edification of the young woman and illuminated the logistical absurdity of her exam room assignment, Belinda was halfway down the hallway on her way to exam room ten.

Belinda and I developed a daily routine early in her rehabilitation period. Riff and I tend to ramble around the house until close to midnight; therefore, we are not early-morning creatures. Around 10:00 A.M. we set out for our morning check on Belinda. I did things for her such as stand around in the bathroom while she took a shower with her balloon-booted foot dangling over the lip at the base of the shower. The only time she could go without that clunky boot was when she slept. We rigged up a way for her to get to and from the bathroom at night without re-ballooning. Dollar General doesn't carry chairs, so I went to the Big Lots store and bought a cheap, lightweight office chair on castors. Keeping the chair beside the bed, Belinda kneels on the chair seat with the bad leg and pushes off with her good foot, like a scooter zipping back and forth to the bathroom. Everything in between she pretty much accomplishes by hopping around. As Belinda has hardwood floors, it works like a charm. She may have to refinish her floors eventually. Hey, I'm ingeniously inventive, but I'm not a magician. It works so well that I've caught her wheeling around her townhome. Anything to avoid cramming her foot into that pneumatic boot. Fortunately, the Lake Manchester Townhomes all have a similar single-level floor plan. Belinda has more furniture strewn about than I do. If a person didn't know better, they would think I came from Amish stock. Actually, I come from my mother's house where knick-knacks were displayed on stupid little tables *everywhere*. I don't have knickknacks anywhere. I don't even display pictures of my family. Nobody cares what my family looks like except my family.

The novelty of Belinda's broken foot quickly faded. With spring in full swing, we were desperate for entertainment. A contingent of advance scouts from the Women's Church Group had been on a month-long mission. The ladies had run out of sites worthy of hauling a busload of church ladies to visit. Belinda volunteered us to ride along on one of the advance scouting missions. I wasn't all that keen on the idea, so I started to make alternate plans.

Fortunately, I saw an interesting column in one of the weekly newspapers about a property on the north end of the Glen that had been purchased and was being prepared for development. Demolition of an old barn—the last outbuilding still standing on the property—was scheduled for Thursday. Engineering feats appeal to us due to the controlled precision of sweaty men operating giant machines. It is very educational.

Blessed with sunny skies and woods filled with blossoming trees, I suggested we take some drinks and sandwiches out to the property and watch the action. The barn was scheduled to be taken down at 1:00 P.M. We were on our way to the site by 11:00 A.M. with our cooler stocked with Diet Coke, plus binoculars, two lawn chairs, and Riff.

"Wouldn't it be cool if they set off those charges where they implode the building?"

"For an old barn? Hardly, Leslie. It's more likely they'll just use bulldozers and dump trucks."

"Still, it's educational watching the men work those machines, huh?"

Following the directions I obtained from the Dekker Company's receptionist, we bumped along a rutted road on the final leg of our journey. "Is all this bouncing around bothering your foot?"

"Nope. I don't know why I can't just chuck this stupid boot."

"Patience, Belinda, patience."

"Patience! Look who's talking."

I aimed a narrow-eyed glare in her direction, and she cracked a smile. As we rolled into a clearing, the massive old barn loomed ominously about three hundred feet away. "Oooooooo, that's a big barn. This may take more than one field trip."

Middle Tennessee has ridiculously high pollen counts in the spring. Each and every type of foliage is in the early stages of flower and leaf development. Trees are sapping and sneezing all over everyone and everything. Each morning there is a layer of pollen floating on top of Lake Manchester like a thin skin of ice. It really is overkill. I wear a silk allergy mask from April through June whenever I have to be outside for any length of time. I never required an allergy mask in Michigan, all *three* weeks of spring and summer.

I slapped my mask over my nose and mouth, hopped out of the car, and approached a couple of very nice-looking young men. They pointed me toward another nice-looking young man who they claimed was the site manager.

The site manager saw me coming and removed his baseball cap as I drew closer. Throwing his hands up in the air, he laughingly drawled (obviously a Tennessean), "Don't shoot, ma'am!"

Everyone's a comedian.

Waving an arm toward the Soul, I introduced myself. "I'm here with my friend Belinda Honeycutt. Belinda has been going stir-crazy because she has been trapped inside a balloon boot for several weeks."

"Balloon boot?" He frowned.

"Yes. It's a torture device engineered by a sadistic orthopedist somewhere that's supposed to cradle your foot in ballooned comfort while one recovers from a broken foot."

The thirty-something man introduced himself as Tully Bledsoe. He grinned. "I see. I can tell by your northern accent you aren't from around here. You must suffer from spring allergies. That would explain the mask. Either that or you plan to rob a liquor store on your way home."

Yes, quite the comedian.

I puffed behind the mask, "Ha-ha. I called your office. We have permission to watch the men work. I promise we won't be a distraction."

We agreed that the best place for Belinda, Riff, and me to set up camp was under some pollinating/sneezing trees a couple of hundred feet away. Hopping behind the wheel, I loosened the mask, allowing it to dangle from one ear. "Belinda, that young man is Tully Bledsoe, the foreman of this operation. He said we can park over there." I pointed toward the agreed-on spot at the edge of a wooded area.

We motored over to our site, and I set about unloading the lawn chairs and cooler. In short order I had Belinda comfortably ensconced on a lawn chair with her discarded balloon boot in the grass beside her, her freed busted foot propped up on a pillow resting on the cooler. With my allergy mask in place, I clipped Riff to her retractable leash, and she promptly sat on Belinda's good foot. We settled in, and I busily worked the binoculars to bring the men, um, barn into focus. It was murder maneuvering around that stupid mask.

Belinda unscrewed the top of a Diet Coke. "This was a good idea."

It was indeed a humongous barn. While observing one talented young man operating a forklift, I mumbled, "If they wait another week or two this barn will probably fall down on its own." He would zoom inside the darkened barn, zoom back out with a load of boards and crap, and then zoom over to the designated dumping site, whirl around, and back in he would go. On a couple of trips he came back out with old stoves and washing machines strapped to the pallet. They had some sort of recycling system going on, because the forklift guy deposited the loads in different Dumpsters. Once he had a gigantic load of lumber, emptying it into what must have been the wood Dumpster. It landed with a *ba-boom!* Monkeying with the focus on the binoculars, I wondered aloud, "I wonder how they take down a barn."

"What? Quit mumbling. I can't hear you behind that surgical mask."

I lowered the binoculars and pinched the mask away from my lips.

"I said, I wonder how they take down a barn." I allowed the mask to snap back into place.

"I thought we agreed they were simply going to knock it down. I realize that explosions would be more exciting, but I doubt we will see any fireworks."

I ceased my binocularity to look at my friend. I enunciated clearly through the silk, "No, I know. I mean, there has to be some kind of methodical manner to bringing down a barn. They won't just ram into the structure willy-nilly. It must be like the lake dredging last summer. The dredger guys had a plan, you know; they mapped out quadrants. They didn't just go dredging around like Pac-Man." I made the Pac-Man-chomping motion with my hand. I swiped at my too-long bangs. "This is interesting. I wish they'd let me inside the barn."

"Oh, that's a good idea. I can just see your feet sticking out from beneath a pile of lumber like the Wicked Witch of the West."

"It was the Wicked Witch of the East that Dorothy flattened. The Wicked Witch of the West was the sister." Again I swiped at my bangs. "I hate this stupid mask. It's annoying."

"At least you don't have to lug around this blasted boot. You need to let Regina cut your bangs. You are never going to make it."

Belinda was right. My bangs have been driving me crazy. I have fine, blond hair that I have *naturally* colored every three weeks. I have worn a modern day version of a Doris Day–style bob for years, and I'm trying for a slight variation by growing out the bangs. They are driving me nuts. Belinda and I frequent the same hairdresser. Neither one of us has a brand name hair color. Regina is a voodoo princess the way she mixes up variations of color.

"I'm trying to grow them out," I said, taking another swipe at them.

"Well, you look like Moe. Quit being so stubborn. Just let Regina cut them."

"Moe?" I snorted from behind my silken veil. "Thanks a lot. The last time Regina mixed up your color, she got too much red in with the brown. Better tell her to take it easy on the red. You told me you wanted Xena, Warrior Princess, not Lucille Ball."

"Better Lucille Ball than one of the Three Stooges." She laughed.

I watched a couple of men back a wrecker inside the barn opening. One was driving the wrecker, and the other was directing. "I wonder what they're hauling out of there that requires a wrecker: an old tractor or something?" I jumped to my feet. I'm going to take Riff for a walk."

"Leslie, don't you go poking around inside that old barn."

"I have no intention of 'poking around' inside that old barn. I only want a closer look." I huffed and set off in the direction of the structure.

"*Leslie*," she called in a warning tone.

Addressing my dog, I said, "She can't come after us with that busted foot."

I had covered half the distance to the site when the wrecker came out of the barn hauling an old car. I ran back to my seated friend shouting with excitement. "Belinda, it's a Nash Rambler. I've got to get a look at this." I one-handed Riff to hold her against my chest, turned on my heel, and ran flat-out toward the old car.

I still hold a grudge against my late father. It involves a 1953 Nash Rambler. When we meet in heaven, I am going to punch him in the nose. Even today I'm not a big person, but when I was sixteen, I was downright scrawny: a skinny little kid with big plans. We had one car. My father was the only one in the family with a driver's license. He was a midlevel executive employed by the state of Michigan. I thought he was the cheapest man in the universe. I now understand my father was frugal out of necessity. Supporting a wife and four children on the salary of a civil servant was a feat of superhuman proportions. Dad drove stripped-down, boxy Fords. Ford Customs to be exact. The cars had all the flash of Elliot Ness's dialogue. Dad paid for an automatic transmission and heat. Any other options were out of the question. He would have declined windshield wipers if he could have saved a buck.

I was determined to get my driver's license, and my father was just as determined that the scrawniest of his three daughters was never going to get her driver's license. I finally passed the road test in that big, old, stupid tank of a car. I needed more pillows than the lead in *The Princess and the Pea* to see over the steering wheel, which, by the way, belonged on a tractor. No power steering and no power brakes—they were options. Turning the car required my full weight dangling from the steering wheel. Braking was a two-footed stomp. Driving that big box at anything more than thirty miles an hour was like driving through sand in a wind tunnel.

When I was seventeen and a high school senior in 1964, I got a job in the file room at a local hospital as part of a co-op class. Transportation to and from the job was hard to arrange, but I managed. One day I saw a small, blue 1953 Nash Rambler in the front yard of a neighbor's house. I was in love. Here was an actual, real-life, Leslie-sized vehicle. The asking price was $135.00. I had been saving my money. I had the money to buy the car. I had the money for the car insurance. If the motor turned over, I was going to buy this car. My father refused to let me purchase the car. He wouldn't even look at it. Since I was under the age of eighteen, I could not buy the car without my father's permission. I never forgot that blue Nash Rambler. I never forgave my father. That car should have been mine.

Belinda called after me, but it was futile. I was jogging toward a wrecker with its hook in the nose of an old, used-to-be-red Nash Rambler. The car limped behind the wrecker on its rear-wheel rims, dusty puffs of rotting tires in its wake. The wrecker stopped, and a winch started slowly lowering the front end to the ground until the old car sat on four flat, shoeless feet. Setting Riff on the ground, I began yanking on the driver's side of the car. I still had the red, plastic leash handle in one hand, so I couldn't get a good grip. I put the handle on the ground and held it in place with my foot. With a massive grunt, the door gave way with a grating, grinding squeal. The leash housing shot out from beneath my foot, and I almost landed on my butt in the dirt. Riff tried to scramble inside the crumbling interior of the vehicle, but I scooped her and the plastic leash housing into my arms. Juggling both, I leaned into the car to explore. The driver of the wrecker came up beside me. "Hey, lady, watch what you are doing there. This old heap has probably been in that barn for more than sixty years! More 'n likely it's full of mice."

That got my attention. I backed away from the car with my dog. Belinda yelled my name, and I glanced in her direction. She was rebooting, energetically pumping up the boot bladders. I watched her get to a rocking stand and start my way. I wouldn't have much time. Either Thad was the name of the man driving the wrecker or he was wearing Thad's shirt: THAD was stitched over the pocket. He was a fit young man maybe in his early twenties. I looked up at him, flicked my right ear free of the elastic doohickey, and spoke around the drooping face mask. "This is a Nash Rambler. Ever heard of the Nash Rambler, Thad?"

Thad shook his head. "No, ma'am. I can tell that it's old though."

"The Nash Rambler was the first American compact car, well, the first one that was successful. It was very popular in the fifties. There was even a song called 'Little Nash Rambler.'" I can't remember it exactly. It went something like 'Beep-beep-beep-beep, his horn went beep-beep-beep.'"

"Uh-huh." I could tell he was less than captivated with my tutorial or my ability to retain inane old song lyrics.

I circled around to the back of the vehicle. Nodding enthusiastically I said, "I was right. This is a Rambler Deluxe." Cradling Riff and her leash in one arm, I patted the top of the vehicle and ran my free hand across the surface. "See here, this is a two-tone model. The deluxe models were all two-tone."

"Doesn't look very deluxe to me." He was right. This was indeed a wreck. The tires were all rotted away, and the body was dented and dirty. Belinda was carefully making her way across the expanse of grass, and Tully Bledsoe had also taken notice that I had taken notice of the old, wrecked vehicle.

Thad had resumed my previous leaning into the car when Tully walked up. A big smile crossed his face. "Hey, it's an old Nash Rambler."

"You're familiar with the Rambler?" I asked eagerly. Riff was wriggling every which way in my arms, so I finally set her on her feet beside me, still tethered to the leash.

Nodding and grinning down at me, Tully boasted, "Shoot, yeah. I go to all the old-car shows in Clifton. This here looks like an early fifties model."

I grabbed Tully's well-muscled arm, tugged him toward the trunk, and pointed at the name scrolled the length of the trunk: R A M B L E R. Beneath the E in Rambler was the identifying word DELUXE. "It's a Rambler Deluxe. Mine was a blue 1953 Country Club Hardtop."

"That right, Mrs. Barrett? You had one of these?"

"Well, not exactly, never mind," I called around the side of the car to Thad, allergy mask swaying beneath my jaw. "Find anything in the car, Thad?"

Dusting his hands together, Thad grinned at me. "Mouse turds, a bunch of old, rusted-out junk—afraid that's about it."

Belinda huffed up behind Thad out of breath. "Leslie, are you boring these gentlemen with your little Nash Rambler story?" Belinda is my best friend in the whole world, so she is familiar with my unresolved grievance against my late father.

I ignored her and asked Tully, "Can we have a look in the trunk? If there is anything of interest in an old, junked car, it's always in the trunk."

Thad nodded. "That's generally the case."

"We don't have a key," said Tully.

Reaching into a back pocket, Thad held up a screwdriver.

"I don't know." Tully was going chicken on me. "This old place belonged to the Madsens. I reckon we would need their permission to break into the trunk."

"Why would they care about this old thing?" I laughed dismissively. "There isn't much left of it. I don't see what harm it would do to open the trunk. Thad's probably right; we'll likely just find a bunch of old mouse poop."

Tully grinned permission at Thad. "What the heck, see if you can get this tin can to pop, Thad."

"Leslie," Belinda warned in her warning voice, "stand back. You could get cut or something."

I moved off a few steps and watched Thad shove the screwdriver into the old rusty lock.

"Jam it in there and twist it around, Thad," I suggested helpfully.

Thad grunted and jiggled the screwdriver, making an awful, screeching racket until we were rewarded with a resounding *thunk*. "Let's see what fortunes we have in here." Thad raised the trunk lid with his right hand and gulped.

"Uh-oh!"

I stepped toward the vehicle flapping dust way from my face. I remasked and huffed through the silk, "What is it?"

Thad and Tully exchanged looks of alarm. Riff backed away to strain at the full length of her leash. "Let *me* see. Let me see." I danced closer.

"No, now, ma'am, you shouldn't." Thad tried to block my view of the trunk with his body.

I made like I was going to go around on his left side—a move my husband used to call a fake in football—and then reversed quickly, ducking underneath his right arm as he held the trunk lid aloft. All I saw was an old, faded quilt, the kind my grandmother used to call a crazy quilt—that is, pieces of fabric from anything and everything sewed together, sort of an anything-goes type of quilt. This one was well used, and all washed out. Then I saw the hand, a skeletonized hand, sticking out from beneath the quilt. I saw the glint of something metallic resting on the quilt and reached for it, coming up with a teensy-tiny key clipped between the thumb and forefinger of my acrylic nails. Thad must have thought I was reaching to remove the quilt because he yelped, "You don't want to do that!" I found myself swept off my feet by a strong arm encircling my waist. Thad swung me around with my back against his hard chest, causing me to drop the handle to Riff's leash. The red plastic housing clattered in the dirt, and Riff went running across the grass away from the Rambler wreck. The red plastic housing bounced crazily through the tall grass. It looked like the leash was chasing the dog.

Thad gazed at the sight. "Ma'am, I believe your dog is the only smart one here."

I hung docilely in Thad's arms. I probably should have struggled or at least complained, but I figured he meant well. Tully caught the trunk lid and eased it down without allowing the lock to engage. Belinda rocked by us in her one-booted stomp, demanding, "What is it? What is in the trunk?" With his arm full of me, Thad couldn't stop her from looking. Tully had already moved off to the side and had a cell phone to his ear. Belinda raised the lid and stared down at the old, faded quilt and the skeletonized hand.

"Well, for heaven's sake, Leslie. You've found another dead body. I wish you would stop doing that. It isn't a competition, you know."

I yelled at Tully, *"Hey, Tully. Get my dog, will you?"* He waved an arm in acknowledgment and jogged after Riff, still holding the phone to his ear.

"Get down from that man," Belinda ordered in her bored/irritated voice.

Thad lowered me to my feet. "Sorry, I probably overreacted. Are you okay now, ma'am?"

I patted his chest. "I'm all right, Thad, but thank you for your chivalry toward a damsel in potential distress. Don't worry about me. I've found dead bodies before—two in fact." I leaned around him to inspect the trunk and frowned to find it mostly closed. Smoothing down my shirt, I surreptitiously slid the discovered key into the back pocket of my soft tailored jeans—my butt still looks pretty good in those jeans.

Eyes wide, he removed his baseball cap and ran a hand through his tousled, sweaty hair. "Two dead bodies?"

"Not at the same time, and *technically*, I can only take credit for *one* dead body. *Technically*, I wasn't the one to find Abner. Did you hear about the old man they scooped up from the bottom of Lake Manchester last summer when they were dredging?"

"I did hear about that. I remember reading that two neighbor ladies kept asking questions until—Wow, you were those two ladies?"

Belinda and I exchanged prideful looks, and I saw her face crinkle in a wince. "Does your foot hurt, Belinda? Do you want me to fetch you a pain pill?"

"No thanks, I'm just tired from chasing after you in this dang boot!"

Thad was grinning. "Yeah, that was something out at Lake Manchester. I volunteer at the fire station in the Glen. Those boys talk about you two all the time. I've told my granddaddy about you. He loves hearing about you. Barrett and Honeycutt, right?"

Belinda laughed. "I don't know if I like the sound of the boys at the firehouse talking about us, Les. Makes us sound like a TV show. *Rizzoli and Isles*... *Starsky and Hutch*... Barrett and Honeycutt... Honeycutt and Barrett."

"*Laverne & Shirley*," I chimed in. We crack each other up.

I turned to my would-be hero, pointed to our abandoned camp site, and puffed through the silk, "Thad, would you do us a big favor? Collect those lawn chairs over there, please. They are those flimsy canvas ones with hollow tubes for legs so they don't weigh anything. There's a cooler with Diet Cokes there too. Bring us a couple, and grab some for your guys. When Tully finishes his conversation with the police, they will descend, and none of us will be going anywhere for a while."

Thad went loping across the grass to collect the chairs and cooler. Belinda again lifted the trunk and stared down at the covered body. Having completed his phone conversation, Tully approached us, handing the red plastic handle to me. Riff was still keeping her distance and glared at me as if to say, "You're going to pay for this one."

Tully ordered, "Don't touch anything, ladies. Our operation is temporarily shut down, and the police don't want anybody to leave. We have a potential crime scene."

"Of course it's a crime scene! What else could it be?" Sometimes when I'm nervous or excited, there is a faucet in my brain that turns on, and inane stories bubble from my mouth, like now. "You know, I read in the newspaper one time in Michigan about this man's body being found in the trunk of a car. Get this; the car had been sunk in a lake, and the guy was tied hand and foot."

Tully shifted his eyes from side to side. "O-o-kay."

"Oh, I left out the best part. According to the news article, the police suspected foul play." I rolled my eyes and hooted. "How stupid is that? What? Did they think the man died an accidental death or committed suicide?" I stabbed a finger at the car in emphasis. "This man obviously did not commit suicide or die of natural causes."

"The chief simply said they would have to investigate to determine whether this man died from an accident of some sort. He's on his way. By the way, he said he knows you two ladies."

I cleared my throat. "Yes, um, we are acquainted with Chief Braddock." I fussed with the elastic encircling my right ear. "This man didn't die as the result of a game of hide-and-nobody-sought. That might be an accidental death for a four-year-old, but the lump underneath that quilt is too large for a child."

Thad came clattering back with the lawn chairs and cooler. I fished out cold diet colas for the four of us and told Tully to invite the rest of the guys to help themselves. I had brought a twelve-pack—Belinda and I love Diet Coke.

When the four of us were slurping our drinks—Belinda and I seated in the lawn chairs, and the guys leaning against the Rambler—Tully nodded his head at Belinda's propped-up, still-booted foot. "What happened?"

I knew he was only making conversation to kill time until Quinn arrived. Dangling mask bouncing around due to my gesticulating hands, I launched into a brand-new narrative. "Belinda broke a bone in her foot playing Pickle Ball. Are you guys' familiar with Pickle Ball?"

Both men shook their heads. Belinda snickered. "Leslie…"

"Pickle Ball is a made-up game. Basically, it's a bunch of racket-type sports rolled into one, like Ping-Pong meets tennis. Anyway, Belinda is superb at Pickle Ball. In fact, she was getting close to playing in a tournament. Unfortunately, she was going for a backhanded swat to the ball at the corner of the table, twisted her foot, and the rest is booted history." I grinned, proud of my latest Belinda's busted-foot story.

"Pickle Ball, eh?" Tully wondered, "What kind of ball do you use for that? I mean, is it a Ping-Pong ball or one of those funny-looking birdie things, like badminton?"

I threw Belinda a look of desperation and, best friend that she is, she jumped in. "What the ball looks like isn't important. What is important is that I get another look at that body."

Tully objected, "I don't think that's a good idea. We should wait for the authorities."

"Belinda was an emergency room nurse in a busy Philadelphia hospital," I announced with pride. "She isn't squeamish at all, and I found a dead body once when I showed up at a lady's house for a home health call. As it turned out, she hadn't been murdered though. We didn't actually find Abner."

"Who's Abner?"

Thad was only too happy to tell the story. "Abner Cummings. You remember hearing about that man last summer who got scooped from the bottom of Lake Manchester out there in the Glen? Mrs. Barrett and Mrs. Honeycutt solved the mystery."

Tully's eyes crinkled at the corners in apparent amusement. "That so?"

Belinda prattled, "We, um, sort of got pulled into the whole mess with Abner. Mr. Bledsoe, I promise I won't touch anything. All I want to do is look to see whether we can determine whether this is the body of a man or woman. Leslie is quite right. The body looks to be the size of an adult."

I preened silently.

"Well, I don't see what harm that could do. Okay. Just don't touch anything." Tully motioned for Thad to raise the lid to the trunk.

We leaned under his raised arm to peer into the trunk. Belinda clicked her eyes around like a stoic medical examiner. I whispered in her ear,

"Why doesn't it stink? Seems like there should be some kind of odor."

Catching my eye over her shoulder she said, "This corpse has been here so long that it has skeletonized. There isn't anything left of him to stink."

"Man, that's sad."

She nodded agreement.

Tully called over to us. "Mrs. Barrett, why is your dog sitting on my foot?"

Without turning, I answered, "She likes you. She wants you to pick her up."

"Oh." Then he said, "Hello, sweetheart. Are you thirsty? Let's get you some water." Belinda and I both glanced his way. He unclipped the leash from her collar and crossed to where the guys had set up a water station of sorts. Setting Riff at his feet, Tully sat on his haunches and turned on the water to fill his cupped hands. Riff looked at the man adoringly, then started lapping water from his calloused hands. There is nothing more macho than a healthy, well-calloused man tending to a thirsty, little-bitty ball-of-fuzz dog.

Turning back to peruse the trunk Belinda made a pronouncement, "This is the body of a full-grown man."

"Wow. You can tell that just by looking at the hand, Belinda? Gee, you're just like that *Bones* lady on TV."

She nodded. "Partly it is because of the hand. The size of the hand suggests it belongs to a man." She nodded again at the end of the quilt. "See that boot down there? That's a large man's boot."

Thad frowned. "You sure that's a full-grown man under that quilt?"

"No doubt he was folded up some to fit in the trunk. It isn't very large."

"After he was dead though. Right, Belinda?" My tone begged for reassurance.

"I certainly hope so."

Tully strode up behind us with Riff in his arms. "This property used to belong to old Cecil Madsen until his son inherited eleven years ago. The son, Denver, died last year. Denver had the old house and other outbuildings torn down long before he died."

Thad added an informational nugget. "Yeah, my granddaddy grew up with Denver Madsen. His daddy was some kind of bank tycoon around here."

I grimaced behind the mask. "I can guess why Denver left the barn intact. He must've known about the surprise in the trunk of the Rambler."

I walked away from the car, poked about for a bit, and returned with a stick.

Belinda snatched it from my hands. "Oh no you don't, Leslie. You do not get to go poking around in this trunk."

"Well, excu-u-use me. I didn't bring my forensic gloves with me today," I barked sarcastically. Turning around, I flicked the elastic doohickey from my ear and hollered into the small crowd of men, *"DOES ANYBODY HAVE A BAGGIE IN THEIR LUNCH PAIL?"*

One young man was already digging through his lunch bag when Belinda yelled with a furious shake of her head, "No...*seriously*...no."

"In a pinch we could use a Baggie in place of a plastic glove."

She shook her head. I grumbled but didn't push my luck.

Thad asked, "Can I close the lid now? My arm is killing me."

"Just a second, Thad." I bounced my eyes around the open trunk, mask swinging beneath my chin. There didn't seem to be anything to see other than the quilt and the guy's boots. So I studied the quilt more closely. I mentally logged pieces of the quilt: squares of denim, pieces of a striped towel, small squares of black poodles, and small squares of white poodles. I mumbled, "I wonder what's up with the poodles."

Thad asked, "What poodles?" I started to answer when Belinda interrupted. "You can close the trunk, Thad, but don't let it latch shut. The cops are here."

# Chapter Five

We heard the approaching vehicles, minus the sirens—the man in the trunk wasn't in a hurry. The Safety Department patrol car pulled up beside the wrecker. PUBLIC SAFETY was emblazoned on the door. Quinn Braddock unfolded from the passenger side of the vehicle. Quinn is a distinguished, silver-haired retired Tennessee state policeman who now serves as the chief of safety for the retirement/resort community of Fairlawn Glen. Officer Mark Edwards climbed from behind the wheel of the car.

I had my silken mask in place as Mark approached. Mark grinned, waggling his fingers in the air in surrender. "Hey there, partner, don't shoot."

Everyone's a comedian.

"I know that's you behind that mask, Mrs. Barrett. It's good to see you; things have been rather boring of late. I asked Quinn if I could come along when I heard you two were out here." Quinn threw Mark an irritated glance.

Everybody gave their account of the story to Quinn, and Mark wrote up a report. I led them through my excitement over the appearance of the old Nash Rambler. I started to babble my Rambler history, but Belinda interrupted. "They don't need to hear about your unrequited love for the 1953 Rambler, Leslie."

"Fine," I harrumphed, cramming my mask in a back pocket. "Anyway, Thad didn't find anything of interest in the vehicle itself, so I suggested we take a peek inside the trunk."

Quinn gave me a vicious scowl before moving on to Thad's account of the events that had followed my suggestion. While they were all talking, I plucked Riff from Tully's arms, muttering something about getting her some more water, which I intended to do, but not before I got a look inside that barn. I clipped Riff's collar to the leash but continued to carry her. I try to be a responsible dog owner, but the little devil is fast.

Belinda could keep me from the trunk, but she'd have to tackle me to stop me from entering the barn. Stepping into the large, shadowy space, I approached two men who were standing around smoking. "It's probably not the best idea to be lighting up in here around all this old hay and dried-out timber. Why don't you just light up a torch and run around playing Olympics?" I scolded. Both men sheepishly dropped their cigarettes and crushed them beneath booted feet.

"Where did you find the Rambler?" I softened my tone.

"The what?" the tall man asked.

"The old car, where did you find the old car?"

The taller man answered, "Oh, back in the far corner there. I wouldn't recommend going back there, lady. This place has been trying to fall down for a lot of years."

"It was just sitting there?"

"This place was filled with junk. Looks like the Madsen family has been using it as a glorified closet for cast-off junk. The car was under a tarp back there, where part of the roof is starting to come down. Thad had to pull it out of there with the wrecker."

"Leslie…what are you doing in there?" Belinda stood backlit in the open door of the barn, hands on her hips. "You're going to get hurt poking around. Come out of there." My best friend in the whole world sometimes thinks she is in charge of me—sometimes it works and sometimes it doesn't. This time I decided she was right.

"Thanks, guys," I called to Tall and Taller, and carried my dog out of the dried-up, dark old barn into the light. "Can we go home now, Belinda? I drank two Diet Cokes, and I have to go to the bathroom."

"Me too. Quinn said we could leave. He called the coroner to come and collect the man in the trunk."

"I hope he plans to involve the TBI for an autopsy and forensic evidence gathering."

"From the looks of that hand, I doubt there's much to autopsy, but, yes, I would imagine that would be the smart thing to do."

I started to walk toward Quinn, but Belinda caught my arm. "Quinn can figure it out on his own, Les. He isn't too happy about us being out here."

That got my back up. "Why? We have every right to watch these men tear down a barn. I called the construction company and everything. The nerve of that man. I'm getting tired of his high-handed ways. Just because he's the chief of police around here doesn't give him the right to tell people where they can and cannot go."

"Whatever you say. Come on, let's go." I could tell from the grimace on my friend's face that her foot was giving her fits, so I decided to leave the investigating to Quinn and Mark.

Thad and Tully helped us stow the lawn chairs and cooler in the Soul. We said our good-byes and drove off down the bumpy, rutted trail. Riff was happily untethered and lapping water from a bowl at Belinda's feet.

Squirming in my seat to lift my rear enough to pluck the balled-up mask from my pocket and toss it onto the backseat. The coroner's van passed as we made our way from what was obviously the scene of a very old murder. The way Riff ran away from that skeleton, she knew it was murder too.

Halfway home I started sneezing.

"Denver Madsen," I muttered around the tissues I held to my leaking nose.

"What's that, Les?"

"Tully said the property used to belong to a Mr. Denver Madsen. Have you ever heard of the Madsen family?"

We were driving south on Trendle Road back into the heart of the Glen. "I've heard of the *Manson* family."

"Very amusing. I'll bet Mrs. Towers has heard of the Madsens."

We were lost in our own thoughts for about five seconds when Belinda snorted a laugh. "Pickle Ball! Where did you come up with that story? I haven't the slightest idea what kind of ball is batted back and forth in that game!"

I pulled into her driveway, laughing along with her. As we were making our way to the front door, Belinda mused, "I wonder why everybody keeps asking me how I broke my foot?"

I shrugged. "They're being polite. Most people don't care how you broke your foot. It's like asking How are you? Watch their eyes glaze over if you start blathering about your arthritis or whatever. Right now I don't care either. I have to go to the bathroom, and I need an allergy pill."

Belinda returned from a visit to the master bathroom. Picking up a growling Butter to deposit him on the floor, she plopped onto the sofa with a grateful sigh. "Help me out of this stupid boot, please."

Butter is the result of an encounter between a female Persian and a feral male. There is nothing wild about Butter. He's long-haired and pretty. Savage, he is not.

Belinda sighed gratefully as I dropped the boot beside the sofa. I moved the secretary chair in front of the sofa for my friend's future mobility, then fetched a couple of Diet Cokes from the fridge. Handing one to Belinda, I sat in the side chair. Riff sat on my foot.

With a nod toward the dog, Belinda said, "Riff is sitting on your foot."

"I know. She's trying to make up for flirting with Tully. It was embarrassing to watch."

Belinda laughed. "You know, Leslie, some people may actually care how I broke my foot."

"Nah, they don't care. We may as well come up with a colorful story. I'm pretty sure you don't want everybody to know how you lost a fight with a Wonderbra in a dressing room at a lingerie store!"

She laughed again. "No, I certainly do not. I should sue those people. Those dressing rooms are way too small for a full-figured woman like me."

"If you are so full-figured, why were you shopping for a Wonderbra?"

We laughed, sipped, and wondered about more than the Wonderbra. "Wonder what happened to that man."

"What man?"

I harrumphed, one-handing Riff onto my lap. "You know *what man*. I suppose we're going to have to wait until after the autopsy to find out how he died. I certainly hope Agent Donnelly is smart enough to impound the car for forensic evidence."

Belinda offered her Coke bottle in a celebratory salute. "And we're off again! If we start poking around in this thing, Quinn Braddock is going to have a fit."

"I don't care what kind of fit Quinn might be inclined to have. We are bored to tears waiting for you to get out of that blasted boot. A little mystery will be good for both of us. Look at it as pure research. We aren't hurting anyone. We'll go over to the Safety Department tomorrow. The man isn't our father, Belinda; and speaking of fathers, we need to develop a cover story. You know, like how my father wouldn't let me buy that Rambler."

"What does that have to do with anything?"

"I'll pretend that I want to buy the barn Rambler. Then work the conversation around to whether or not the TBI has the vehicle. Obviously the man was murdered."

"Nobody knows that the man was murdered, Les."

"Yeah, right, the man decided to take a little snooze inside the locked trunk of a broken-down old Rambler."

She smiled slyly. "Well, he *was* covered with a quilt."

I snorted. "Uh-huh, and then somebody covered said busted old Rambler with a thick, heavy tarp and wedged the whole mess into the far corner of an old barn. The real problem here is that I don't know whether Agent Hailey Donnelly is smart enough to recognize foul play when she sees it. Just like the stupid police in Michigan."

Belinda smacked the palm of her hand against her forehead. "Darn it, Les. We can't go tomorrow. We're going with the church ladies to check out that old manor house."

"Shoot. Let's cancel the manor house."

She shook her head. "Can't. I promised Maria Tuff we'd go. She's having a hard time getting anybody to accompany her on those scouting missions. I thought a little trip would break up the boredom. I had no way of knowing you were going to find another dead body."

"Okay, I guess the man in the trunk can wait for one more day."

# Chapter Six

Spring was shaping up nicely. Belinda's broken foot is the most exciting thing that has happened since the beginning of hunting season. Belinda and I uncovered some seriously nasty characters at Sam Tackett's place this past October. Since then Fairlawn Glen has been peacefully boring. Except for that one night in the middle of November when some teenage hoodlums made a return appearance in the middle of the night, whooping and hollering through our twenty-unit complex. I had encountered these cretins over the summer, roaring around on four-wheeled machines, bashing mailboxes and carriage lamps. They got away from me the first time. This time eighty-seven-year-old Larry Conroy erupted from Unit 8 and let loose a couple of shotgun blasts into the sky.

*BLOOEY...BLOOEY!* It scared the you-know-what out of those kids. They were quickly rounded up by Chief Braddock. The next day Larry told me Braddock gave him some crap about recklessly shooting off the firearm at a bunch of kids. Larry explained to the chief that he had only sent warning shots into the sky with his duly registered shotgun, exactly as Vice President Joe Biden instructed law-abiding citizens to do when overrun with hoodlums. Objecting to advice from the vice president is hard.

Since Belinda had promised that we would ride along on the scouting mission, we pulled into the church parking lot the following morning at 9:00 A.M. I wasn't happy about the early hour or the planned activities.

I almost didn't go when I found out that the old manor house was a good hour's drive away. I definitely wouldn't have tagged along if I had known Maria Tuff was going to be doing the driving. Maria has rheumatoid arthritis. The woman doesn't put up with pain. When one of her joints starts acting up, she heads to the hospital, where they slap in a new one and away she goes. Last Christmas she tumbled down the stairs at her daughter's house like a tossed sock monkey. I lost count of how many replacement joints had to be re-replaced that time. The woman has so many screws and wires holding her together she could be an entire aisle at Home Depot.

"Oh man, you didn't tell me Maria was going to drive. What if she gets the sudden urge to pull over at one of those scenic overlook places and one of her valves or pistons blows? I hate those places anyway. I know what air looks like."

"Hush. You'll be in the backseat with Cory Lynn. It's a comfortable car, and Maria's just fine. She's on pain medicine. All you have to do is ride."

"Great. She's is all gimped up *and* on drugs. How come I have to ride in the back?"

"Because I have a broken bone, a balloon boot on my foot, and I'm on drugs. I get the front passenger seat."

"Great. The doped-up cripples get to ride in front. That's discrimination of some kind. Maybe you should go without me, Belinda. I'm not so sure Riff will be okay with Mrs. Towers. When Mrs. Towers forgets a beauty shop appointment, something is seriously wrong."

Last week Lilly called Belinda because Mrs. Towers hadn't shown up for one of her three weekly beauty shop appointments, and she wasn't answering the phone. Belinda sent me to check on our more-elderly-than-we-are neighbor. I trotted down to Unit 19 and *yoo-hoo*ed through the front door. She was in her bedroom watching a rerun of

*The Andy Griffith Show*. The one in Mayberry with Opie and Aunt Bee.

"She said she never heard the phone ringing, and the appointment with Lilly 'slipped her mind.' Mrs. Towers does not *slip* when it comes to her hair or gossip. She loves a good mystery as much as we do. Yet she didn't so much as bat an eye when I told her about finding the skeleton. I'm telling you, there's something wrong with the woman."

"I agree with you, Les—you know that I do. That's why I called her daughter in Cincinnati. Valerie said she would follow up with her mother's doctor. Mrs. Towers is getting more and more forgetful. I felt Valerie needed to know we're concerned."

"Maybe I should stay home today. She may not be up to taking care of Riff."

"Riff will be okay. We're only going to be gone for three or four hours. Mrs. Towers loves to babysit Riff."

The first person to inquire how Belinda had injured her foot had been Mrs. Towers. When I started in on a new version of the accident, Belinda did a double take. She had been expecting the gum-in-the-parking-lot story. Instead, I launched into a new narrative that I made up on the spot. "You should have been there, Mrs. Towers. We were shopping at Belk, and you know how I hate to shop, so Belinda was shopping, and I was watching people. I saw some woman stuff a blouse into her purse, hanger and all. I hollered, '*Somebody stop that lady! She just stole a blouse!*' You know how quick Belinda can be. Well, she took off after that shoplifter at a dead run. When they got to some stairs, the woman vaulted all three steps with Belinda close behind. Unable to clear the stairs, Belinda smacked the arch of her foot against the edge of the second step!" I made a vicious chopping gesture with my hand. "Down she went!"

"Leslie, if you don't want to tell me how Belinda broke her foot, just say you don't want to tell me."

"We don't want to tell you how Belinda broke her foot."

"Fine…then I won't ask again." Mrs. Towers has asked me three more times how Belinda broke her foot. Each time I make up a new story. The only part of the story that remained the same is my dislike of shopping.

There was another part of this scouting expedition I wasn't thrilled about. Lunch was to be included in the price of a tour of the manor home. I'm no dummy. Whenever you mention a lunch trip with a bunch of women, there will be some shopping somewhere. I allowed myself to be strapped into the backseat along with Cory Lynn. Cory Lynn is a perfectly nice lady, but I know absolutely nothing about the woman. I hoped she wasn't expecting small talk. I don't do small talk. I'm sixty-nine. Any talking time I have left in life is only going to be about big stuff.

The trip took three and a half hours, after which we declared the old manor house to be an old manor house with old manor house period furniture, and not worth a Women's Church Group field trip. If you've seen one old manor house with flowered love seats and claw-foot tubs, you've pretty much seen them all. Lunch was crappy, but the souvenir shop was a big hit—told you so.

When we returned to the church, I opened my car door and jumped down to the pavement singing, "Bye, girls! It was fun!" I ran around the Escalade to collect my best friend. Maria was saying something nice to Belinda, but she was no longer listening. The dream of a nice outing with church lady friends had turned into stomping around an old manor house, eating a chicken salad sandwich on a week-old, chewy croissant, and all the pain in the world draining into her foot.

# Chapter Seven

By the time I wheeled into Belinda's driveway, my friend was writhing in pain from intense boot encapsulation. She had wanted to take the boot off when we left the manor, but I was afraid she'd never get the stupid thing back on. I had visions of us playing Roller Derby in her driveway with the secretary chair. Now she was mad at me because her foot was on fire.

It was almost a rerun of our return from the hospital, only this time I led the way into the house, with Belinda rocking along behind me. The moment she slammed the front door Belinda shrieked, "Gosh darn it all, my freaking foot is killing me!" Belinda's shriek can shake your fillings loose.

Taking control of the situation—which is what we professional social workers are trained to do—I barked an order, "Sit down on the couch and start de-ballooning that contraption. I'll get some ice for your foot and a glass of water. Take two of your pain pills this time. And *stop yelling*. That stupid trip wasn't my idea."

By the time I came hustling into the living room with a Baggie of ice in one hand and a glass of water in the other, Belinda was practically in tears trying to release the balloon-boot bladders. I gave her the water and ordered, "Fish two pain pills out of your purse. I'll get the boot off."

"F-fank you," she snuffled. Hurt feet hurt like the devil on a hot day. As the balloons were deflating, she started huffing, "*Ow-ow-ow*."

I pulled the clunky boot off her foot and told her to slide back onto the couch and put both feet up. "I have to go to the ba-f-f-room" she wailed pitifully.

"I'll help you in a minute. For now, swing around and put your feet up."

She did as I instructed while gulping down two pain pills. I laid an afghan over her foot and gently eased the bag of ice against the arch of her foot.

She leaned back and snuffled, "Would you please get me some tissues or something?"

I zipped back into the kitchen and returned with a roll of paper towels. "I'm going down to Mrs. Towers' to get Riff. You relax for a few minutes. I'll be right back."

I congratulated myself on how well I was handling this latest crisis. Passing Abner's old unit on my way to Unit 19, I felt a rush of sadness. There was a FOR SALE/PENDING sign in the upstairs window. Sadness was quickly replaced with excited curiosity over the pending sale. I quickly forgot all about Abner as a brown UPS truck zipped past and into the driveway of Unit 7. This is an ongoing mystery at Lake Manchester Townhomes. Hardly a day goes by when Mrs. Farrow in Unit 7 doesn't receive a package from UPS, FedEx, or the US Postal Service, sometimes all three. It's very curious. Parcels literally pile up on the woman's porch.

I stood by the driver's side of the delivery truck waiting for UPS guy to gallop back to his truck. I cleverly vocalized an observation, "Boy, Mrs. Farrow sure does get a lot of packages, doesn't she?"

The guy mumbled, "Excuse me, ma'am, I'm on a tight schedule." I stepped back to allow him to open the door and slide behind the wheel. You don't mess around with a UPS driver and his/her schedule. I don't know what I was expecting him to say in response to my astute observation. There are probably all kinds of confidentiality rules about that sort of thing. I can't believe the delivery people don't wonder what in the heck is going on with Mrs. Farrow. Maybe one day I can get a blabbermouth driver to spill the beans, maybe.

Something like: Mrs. Farrow's grandson grows marijuana on rooftops in Manhattan, cuts the leggy plants into smoke-sized pieces, then ships the results to his grandmother in various boxes that he has collected for this specific purpose. He is a bright boy, a veritable genius, shipping his illegal gains in boxes bearing the logos of Zappos Shoes, The Vermont Country Store, Chico's, and the like. After Grandmother Farrow tokes through her share of the harvest to combat some terrible illness, such as glaucoma, she sells the remainder of the Manhattan marijuana crop to some guy who goes by the name of Claude.

This is where I always lose the thread of the story. Reminding myself that I was on my way to collect my dog, I walked the length of the complex and *yoo-hoo* my way through Mrs. Towers' front door. I was met with silence. No yapping little dog that treats my sudden reappearance into her life as a delightful magic trick. No singsong voice of Mrs. Towers accompanied by the sound of her walker swishing across the carpet.

Silence.

"Mrs. Towers? Riff?"

Nothing.

I started to search, fully expecting to find Mrs. Towers tangled up in her walker somewhere on the premises. That wouldn't explain Riff's silence. I couldn't find either one of them anywhere in the house. A quick peek in the garage verified that her car was there. I snagged her help-gizmo from a TV tray in the living room, then I saw the walker parked in the dining room.

I ran to the telephone and called Belinda. It took her forever to answer with an irritated "Hello."

"Belinda, it's me."

"Leslie, I had to hop all the way into the kitchen to answer the phone. You left me stranded on the couch with my secretary chair in the bedroom. As long as I'm up, I'm going to hop into the bathroom."

I interrupted her crabby protestations. "I can't find Mrs. Towers or Riff anywhere. Her walker is parked in the dining room, and her help-gizmo was lying on a TV tray in the living room. Her car is in the garage."

"Is her ATV gone?" Mrs. Towers has a sturdy black walker-type thing with tires and a padded seat that flips down to allow a walker-dependent person to rest. We call it her all-terrain vehicle, or ATV for short.

I ran around with the cordless phone at my ear panting, "I don't see it. Where could she have gone? What should I do?" Just a few minutes ago I was all take charge when Belinda was in jeopardy. But, hey, this is my dog.

"Mash the button on the help-gizmo."

"But I don't know where she is."

"Leslie…mash the button. The help-gizmo people will send help. She could have gone off into the woods or something. Go ahead and mash the button."

I mashed the button, and nothing happened. "Nothing happened, Belinda."

"Well, it isn't a magic button, Leslie. Wait a minute."

"What, what?"

"Be quiet."

"Why?"

"Leslie, I think I hear Riff barking."

"Where? Where is she?"

"I'm not sure. Come on back. I'm sure I hear her barking."

I disconnected the call and ran out the front door carrying the help-gizmo. I could hear the telephone ringing in the house and figured it was the help-gizmo people. Good. As I jogged closer to Belinda's place, I heard Riff's animated barking and followed the sound to Abner's front door. Yanking on the door, I found it unlocked. Riff's frantic barking was coming from the garage.

Mrs. Towers was sitting in the middle of Abner Cummings' empty garage on her flipped-down ATV seat. Riff had circled her so many times Mrs. Towers looked like a tied hostage. Unclipping Riff from her leash, I swept my sweet dog into my arms, crying, "Mrs. Towers, what in the world are you doing?"

She looked up at me with tearful eyes. "Leslie, I can't find Abner anywhere."

# Chapter Eight

We had to delay our trip to the Safety Department because of the Mrs. Towers' emergency. Lab results revealed a severe vitamin B12 deficiency. I had seen it before when I worked in the nursing home, and then later on in home health. A simple B12 deficiency can cause weight loss, anemia, and confusion, all the symptoms our neighbor has been manifesting for several weeks. It was a relief to learn the problem was something that could be fixed with injections, a daily vitamin regimen, and improved dietary habits. She stayed in the hospital until her B12 levels was close to normal, and then Valerie had her transferred to a skilled nursing facility.

Belinda and I visited Mrs. Towers once she was safely transferred to The Clifton Living Well Center, commonly known as the Clifton Nursing Home. It's silly how corporations monkey with the name of a place in an attempt to sugarcoat its reality. It sure looked like a nursing home to me. It did to Mrs. Towers too, and she was fit to be tied about the whole thing. With the rapid return of her mental faculties, she was mad and mean. Valerie couldn't take it and hightailed it back to Cincinnati, claiming she had to get back to work. The little-girly coward.

I'd been dying to bring up the skeleton in the trunk again and quiz Mrs. Towers about the Madsen family. Belinda made me keep quiet until we were confident that her B12 deprived brain had returned to normal. One week into her nursing home stay we were finally on our way to The Clifton Living Well Center to visit Mrs. Towers and pump her for information about the Madsen clan.

On entering the building, a purse lady zipped across the lobby. Every nursing home has one or two purse ladies. The elderly woman was dressed nicely in a church-going dress, hair styled and sprayed into presentable form. She carried a purse in the crook of one arm. At first glance she looked like everybody else visiting a nursing home. When I looked into her rumpled eyes, I knew she had some type of dementia.

The purse lady stopped us in the hallway. "Excuse me. Have either of you ladies seen Mitch Turley?"

Belinda and I shook our heads. The purse lady turned abruptly and went striding down the hall with purposeful, determined steps, intent on a destination within the hallways of her mind. Her voice carried down the hall. "Excuse me. Have you seen Mitch Turley?"

Entering Mrs. Towers' room, it was immediately evident that our friend was in full control of her mental faculties.

"Thank the Lord! Girls, get me the #&&% out of here!"

We settled in for a visit, and I asked, "When is the doctor planning on releasing you?"

"To #&&% with the doctor. I'd climb out a window if I could get to my walker."

Belinda pointed to the walker sitting beside the bed. "Your walker is right there."

Mrs. Towers sighed mightily. "I know, but I poop out after about three steps."

"You need some physical therapy," Belinda announced. "You're weak from bed rest."

Mrs. Towers thumped a fist on the mattress and shouted, "Well then, get me some $%#@ physical therapy!"

Belinda immediately spat back at her, "Stop cursing all over the place. Obviously, you're in control of your mental faculties; tell one of the nurses to contact your doctor and get an order for PT to combat the weakness."

In a soft, sufficiently chastised voice, Mrs. Towers asked, "Belinda, would you please ask one of those nurses out there to come in, please?"

"No problem." Belinda left the room with a dignified huff.

"She's right, you know. You've got to move it or lose it. You need to take better care of yourself at home. Stop wandering around without your help-gizmo. One of these days we're going to find you buried beneath fifty snow globes. And you need to eat better too."

Mrs. Towers huffed, "You should talk, Leslie Barrett! You live on Diet Cokes, Belinda's coffee, and grilled-cheese sandwiches!" She had a point there. Still, she reluctantly admitted I had made a few valid points as well.

"Can you make it to the bathroom on your own?"

"I try, but I'm too shaky. They make me use that contraption." She nodded toward the bedside commode.

Belinda returned with a young nurse. "How can I help you, Mrs. Towers?"

Mrs. Towers repeated word for word what I had just coached her to say. "I want to go home, but I need to get my strength back. Please contact my physician and request an order for physical therapy. I live alone and need to build up my endurance so I can safely return to my home."

"Of course, Mrs. Towers. Once I connect with our social worker to arrange any services you may require at home, I will put in a call to the doctor's office and let you know the outcome." With that the nurse exited the room.

I alerted Mrs. Towers to what I was sure would follow. "Be prepared for the facility social worker to pay you a visit very soon."

"Why?"

"I'm psychic. Plus, I worked in a nursing home. I know the system."

A well-modulated voice asked from the doorway, "Pardon me, but have you seen Mitch Turley?" It was the purse lady.

Mrs. Towers called out to the woman, "No, dear."

The purse lady turned and disappeared into the hallway.

Looking at the empty doorway, I said, "She has some form of dementia. Who's she looking for?"

Mrs. Towers met my gaze with surprise and appreciation. "I keep forgetting you used to work with older folks. Yes, that lady is Mrs. Ruth Turley. I'm told she has Alzheimer's. All the poor thing does all day is walk around asking people whether they have seen Mitch Turley. Mitch Turley was her husband. From what the aides told me, he died six months ago. Mrs. Turley keeps forgetting. I cringe every time I hear a member of the staff correct her. It seems cruel to keep telling her that he's dead. She gets so upset."

"Come with me, Belinda." I headed for the door and tossed over my shoulder, "We'll be right back, Mrs. Towers. I want to speak with someone about Mrs. Turley."

Belinda started to object—"We shouldn't get involved"—but followed me from the room. I looked up and down the hallway until I saw Mrs. Turley in the arms of a forty-something woman who was doing her best to console her. I stopped one of the nurse aides as she passed with a stack of linens. "Excuse me, who is that woman with Mrs. Turley?"

The young woman answered quickly, "Oh, that's her daughter, Liz."

I thanked the young woman, and she hurried off with her linens. I walked determinedly down the hall and spoke assertively to Ruth Turley. "Mrs. Turley." I jiggled her arm to gain her attention, and she turned her weepy eyes toward me. "Hi, Mrs. Turley. My friend here can't find the front entrance. Would you please show her where it is?"

Belinda and the daughter looked at me with puzzled expressions. Mrs. Turley abruptly beamed at Belinda. "Of course, dear, I'd be glad to show you where it is." She patted her daughter's hand. "I will be right back, Liz. I have to help this lady." Off she went with her purse in the crook of one arm, her other arm linked with Belinda's.

Looking at me bewildered, the daughter asked, "Excuse me, what was that all about?"

I quickly introduced myself and explained I had a professional background working with Alzheimer's patients. "How long has your mother been a patient here?"

"Why?"

"Look, Liz, we don't have a lot of time; just tell me quickly how your mother ended up here."

Guilt is never far away from the adult child of a parent with dementia. Liz said, "Mother has been here for a little over a year. As long as Daddy was well, he and Mother did okay at home. Then when he started getting sick, we admitted Mother here hoping it would be temporary, but…Daddy got worse." Her eyes filled with tears. "I have a husband and family of my own to care for." The ever-present guilt was in her voice.

"Do you get frequent calls from the staff to come over here and try to calm your mother?"

"Oh yes. I can't keep running up here. I have a job; I have a family."

"Liz, your mother can't hold on to the reality of your father's death. It's cruel to keep telling her that he's dead."

Liz' eyes rounded. "It feels that way to me too. Then again, it isn't right to lie to her."

I shook my head in disgust. "When your mother asks staff members if they've seen Mitch, they don't have to lie to her. They should just respond by saying something like, 'No, Mrs. Turley. I haven't seen him lately.' It would be technically true, and would satisfy her without upsetting her over and over again. It's called redirection."

I saw only relief as she nodded tearfully. "Yes, that makes sense to me. When Mother asks where my father is, I should say something like, 'I don't know what Daddy is doing today, probably visiting with friends.' Which could be the heavenly truth. Is that what you mean?"

I nodded happily. "Yes, and maybe ask her to retell a favorite story about your father, that kind of thing. Your mother will be happier, and it will take a lot of stress and undeserved guilt from your heart. This approach is called validation therapy. Ask to her doctor about it."

I could hear Belinda talking loudly to her new friend as they walked to the building's entrance. Liz leaned in close, whispering, "I can't thank you enough."

Belinda sang out as they approached, "We're back!"

"Oh good," I sang in return. "Thank you so much, Mrs. Turley. We appreciate your help. We have to go back and visit with our friend. I'm sure we'll see you around." I waved in farewell.

As we walked back to Mrs. Towers' room, we heard Ruth Turley ask her daughter in an irritated tone, "What is keeping your father?"

I smiled at Liz' reply: "I don't know, Mom, but knowing Daddy, he can't wait to see you."

Good girl.

We had only been gone fifteen minutes before we got back to Mrs. Towers' room. An attractive young woman was in her room. Mrs. Towers' face was a dark cloud forecasting severe weather up ahead. We introduced one another all around. The lady was Karen, the facility social worker.

Speaking directly to Belinda and me, Karen said, "I understand you requested PT orders from Mrs. Towers' physician."

Mrs. Towers sat straight up in the bed. "Young lady, *I* requested PT orders be obtained from my physician. I'm tired of lying around here. I need to get my strength back so I can go home."

The prim lady quoted from the nursing home social worker playbook that still interferes with my sleep. "It's my understanding that your daughter has power of attorney. I've spoken with Valerie by phone. She is looking into assisted living facilities in Cincinnati. Actually, we have a lovely wing right here for our assisted living residents."

I'm sure you do.

A tirade about nursing homes taking hostages in order to bill Medicare and private insurances up the wazoo, not to mention the private-pay dollar signs that perpetually dance before the eyes of the corporate folks on the board of directors, was on the tip of my tongue.

Mrs. Towers beat me to it. "Karen, I granted my daughter power of attorney, not guardianship. I am of sound mind. My B12 and electrolytes are no longer out of whack. You and Valerie can look at all the assisted living facilities you want. Go ahead, knock yourselves out. My husband and I moved from Ohio twenty years ago. He's gone now, but I still have the home we made here in Tennessee. I'll give you people one or two more days. Then I'm going home. I suggest you tell them to hurry up with those PT orders so we can get started."

It was a magnificent speech. Anyone who doubted Mrs. Towers' mental acuity before would not do so now. I inserted, "Karen, Mrs. Honeycutt and I live in the same complex as Mrs. Towers. She will not be alone. I suggest you call Valerie and give her that assurance."

"I'll call Valerie myself, Leslie," Mrs. Towers snapped.

"Sorry, Mrs. Towers, of course, you will." I felt sufficiently chastised.

With that out of the way, we helped Mrs. Towers to the bathroom and back. She was as shaky as a bowl of Jell-O but settled back into the bed with a grin of accomplishment. She wanted to know all about Mrs.

Turley. When I repeated my conversation with Mrs. Turley's daughter, Belinda shook her head. "I hope that was the right thing to do, Leslie."

"Of course, it was."

We stayed with Mrs. Towers long enough to tell her about finding the man in the trunk of the Rambler out at the old Madsen place. "There was a skeleton in the trunk?" Mrs. Towers all but clapped her hands. "Oh, Leslie, that is delightfully awful. Why didn't you tell me?"

"We did tell you. All you did was give us that vitamin deficiency stare of yours."

"Oh dear. I've been missing all the fun, haven't I?"

"Oh, guess what else we just found out?"

"What?!"

"Abner's daughter sold his unit. The new owner's name is Carmella O'Keefe. According to Lenore Conroy—you know Lenore, Larry's wife. They live in Unit 8. Lenore has that big nose that takes up three-quarters of her face."

"Yes, Leslie, I know Larry and Lenore."

"Well, I called Lenore last night. According to Lenore, Mrs. O'Keefe is a young Italian widow. She's only fifty-three. She has long, black hair and those smoky eyes that Italian women are known for. She said we're likely going to lose the rest of the men in the complex to heart failure, that is, if Larry's response to the woman is any indication." I laughed. "Lenore said Larry's pulse still hasn't normalized!"

Belinda shook her head at us and rolled her eyes. "You're both nosy and just plain weird."

"Yes, we know." Mrs. Towers and I answered in unison, which caused all three of us to laugh.

Mrs. Towers didn't know anything about Cecil Madsen or his family. We left her with instructions to see what she could find out from Lilly, Clifton hairdresser and gossip extraordinaire.

"We're going to stop by the Safety Department for an update before we go home. We'll check in with you tomorrow. You concentrate on getting your strength back, Mrs. Towers. Work the telephone with Lilly, and anyone else you can think of; we need you."

# Chapter Nine

Ipicked up Riff at the reception desk. Because she isn't a certified therapy dog, they wouldn't allow Riff to visit with Mrs. Towers in her room. Another grievance Mrs. Towers has with the place. On our way through the parking lot and back to the Soul, Belinda said, "You do know that everything you muscled your way into back there concerning Mrs. Turley was absolutely none of your business."

I slid behind the wheel of the car. Once buckled in, I started the ignition and turned to my friend. "I'm a social worker. When I encounter emotional suffering, it's my professional duty to interfere. You're a nurse. If you came across somebody bleeding on the sidewalk, you would try to help. Mrs. Turley and her daughter were bleeding."

Belinda stroked Riff's ears. "Actually, I was proud of you. *But*, it still wasn't any of your business."

"I don't care."

On the way home we stopped by the Safety Department. Officer Mark Edwards welcomed us with a broad grin and announced our arrival in a voice loud enough to carry over the cubicle walls and into the office area. "Hello, Mrs. Barrett and Mrs. Honeycutt. What can we do for you today?"

I grinned at Mark and whispered, "Do you think he heard you?"

Quinn Braddock appeared through the make-believe doorway—it's actually just a break between two cubicle walls. I find it amusing that our Safety Department is made out of Legos. Quinn approached with a grim look on his handsome face and all but snarled, "To what do we owe this pleasure?"

"Don't be such an old poop, Quinn," I quipped. "I've always wanted a Nash Rambler. It's a leftover dream from my adolescence. I was wondering whether that Rambler we found is for sale."

"You did not *find* that Rambler, Mrs. Barrett. Besides, that car is a rusted-out old heap. Agent Hailey Donnelly arranged for her forensic experts to go over it."

"That was the correct thing to do." I nodded smartly. "Do you know what they found?"

"The TBI will be relieved to know you concur with their procedures. And Agent Donnelly is under no obligation to keep me apprised of forensic evidence."

"You're being an old poop again, Quinn."

"He can't help himself," Belinda said mockingly. Mark barked a laugh. Quinn glared him into silence.

Quinn softened. "I'm sorry to sound so abrupt, ladies. To be quite honest, it concerns me that I keep finding the two of you in potentially dangerous situations. That old barn should've been torn down a long time ago. Thad Marshall had no business prying that trunk open either."

"Don't blame Thad for that. I encouraged him to pry it open. At the time it seemed like the right thing to do. There could've been wads of cash or old, moldy drugs in that trunk."

"True, but it wasn't your property; nor was it your business."

Belinda swallowed a laugh. "Quinn, eventually someone would have opened that trunk. What difference does it make *who* did it? When we discovered the body, we didn't disturb anything."

I cringed inwardly. I had completely forgotten about the key still in the pocket of my makes-your-butt-looks-good pants at home.

Quinn nodded. "Yes, that's also true. The car would have been towed to the boneyard owned by the Marshall family, and the trunk would have been opened there."

I frowned. "What's a boneyard?"

Belinda leaned over and said softly, "'Boneyard' is a euphemism for a place where old cars go to die, Leslie. You know, a salvage yard."

"This case belongs in a boneyard, wouldn't you agree, Quinn? There wasn't anything left of that poor soul in the trunk except for bones."

Quinn ran his hands through his hair. "When you start talking like that, I get concerned."

"Talking like what?"

"*Case*. This is not a *case* for anyone other than the TBI. This entire *case* is in their hands. What were you girls doing out there at the old Madsen place anyway?"

"We were there to watch the barn deconstruction. I called the company for permission beforehand and everything. Belinda broke her foot and is going loony with boredom. It seemed like a potentially entertaining, safe outing. It was safe; Belinda and I are perfectly fine. Riff got a little squirrelly there for a while, but even she's okay now." I held Riff to my face. "Right, Riff?" She licked my nose, which I hate.

Quinn glanced at Belinda. "How did you break your foot?"

I opened my mouth to spin some outrageous story, but Belinda cut me off. "I assure you it was nothing even remotely spectacular or suspicious."

Tongue in cheek, Mark asked, "You sure you weren't injured while in mad pursuit of escaping felons?"

I like Mark. He was a congenial compatriot during the entire fiasco out at Sam Tackett's place. The man knows how to have fun. Quinn—although ruggedly handsome in a war-weary-cop sort of way—has way too much respect for the law in my opinion. I mean, this is Fairlawn

Glen, a retirement community, not Chicago.

We were seated comfortably at Belinda's place, and, having consumed our grilled-cheese sandwiches, my friend asked why the Rambler had meant so much to my teenage self.

"It was small, like me. I had saved up the money for it. I even loved the name: Rambler. I envisioned myself rambling about the country like a carefree vagabond in my little compact car."

"You don't like to travel, Leslie."

"Well, I didn't know that then; I was seventeen. Nobody knows what they like to do when they're seventeen."

"You aren't actually considering buying that old Rambler, are you?"

"Of course not! Why would I want that piece of junk?"

# Chapter Ten

I hung around Belinda's place until almost 2:00 P.M. I get antsy if I sit for too long. She was snoozing on the sofa courtesy of one pain pill. I had a great idea, but I knew my friend wouldn't approve, so I didn't tell her. Riff danced beside me all the way to the front door.

"Shhhhhh, Riff." I eased out the front doorway and walked briskly to my unit. Riff lagged behind for bathroom purposes. Once both of us were inside, I went into my bedroom, dug through the laundry basket for the jeans, and fished the key from the pocket. It was a regular old silver key, nothing magic or anything. It was less than two inches long and had a circular end for finger-holding-on-to. The business end was straight with one jagged tooth jutting at the end. It reminded me of an old-timey type key. What it was for, I had no idea. I turned it over in my hand and squinted at the knobby end. I was able to make out an engraved *T*, then a scratched space where a letter used to be, followed by two *R*s. Scratched beneath the letters was the number 48.

I scribbled a note for Belinda: "I'm heading out to the old Madsen place to have another look at the barn. Don't worry. I found this key on the corpse. See what you can find on the Internet." Returning to Belinda's, I deposited Riff in my vehicle, then slipped inside the townhouse (where she was still napping) and left the note and key on the seat of the secretary chair where she'd be sure to find it.

Happy to be doing something constructive, I bounced down the dirt road to the old Madsen barn. Passing the foundation where the house had once stood, I realized how far the barn had been from the house. When I drove into the clearing, I spotted a sedan with a State of Tennessee emblem on the side. Parking beside the vehicle, I slipped on my silk mask and clipped Riff to her retractable leash.

Slamming the car door, I whirled to face the barn.

"Well, well, well, Mrs. Barrett." She held up her hands in surrender. "Don't shoot."

Everyone's a comedian.

Agent Hailey Donnelly walked toward me. "I wondered how long it would take for you to show up."

I released my mask from one ear and greeted her with a casual wave. "Hailey, hi. I, um, didn't realize the barn deconstruction had been halted."

Hailey is a TBI agent. Belinda and I had gotten to know her quite well over the past year. It seems as if every time we turn around, we're right in the middle of a TBI investigation. Hailey is slender, with shoulder-length dark-blond hair. Her height falls somewhere between Belinda and me; five feet five or so.

Riff, panting, jumped around Hailey. She's under the impression that God put every human being on this earth solely for her entertainment. The last time Belinda and I spoke with Hailey, we hadn't parted on the best of terms. I decided to be mature and stuck out my hand instead of my tongue. "Sorry about last October, Hailey. No hard feelings I hope." She returned the handshake, but bristled like a cat when I added, "You and your agents would have figured out what was going on out at Sam Tackett's place eventually."

Dropping my hand, she stuck her nose in my face. "Look, Leslie…" Before she could finish, a man emerged from the dark recesses of the barn.

I jumped. "Oh my goodness! You startled me."

Abandoning Hailey for the newcomer, Riff spun toward the newest voice like a whiffle ball in play.

Hailey's lips formed a pinched, thin line. "Leslie Barrett, this is Agent Don Huddleston."

Shooting Hailey a curious look, I diverted my eyes to the young man, and we shook hands. He squatted down to run a hand over Riff's ears. Hailey scowled at him. She was ticked about something. I shrugged it off as her problem. She's a touchy woman.

"You shut down the barn deconstruction." I nodded my approval. "A good move while you gather potential evidence. Have you identified the body yet?"

Hailey rocked to her tiptoes and back again. "Yes, yes, we have made a positive identification."

"And?"

"And what, Mrs. Barrett?"

I splayed my hands in frustration. "And, who is he? What is the dead man's name? How long has he been in that trunk?"

Her eyes narrowed. "How did you know the body in the trunk was the body of a man?"

I replied in my best talking-to-a-dummy voice, "Because he was a man when I stuck him in that trunk, ha-ha. Belinda saw his boots sticking out from beneath the blanket. Great, big, honking-sized boots."

Agent Huddleston stood to address me over Hailey's shoulder. "Your friend is pretty observant, Mrs. Barrett."

I liked the looks of this guy. He reminded me of Bruce Willis, the thirty-something *Die Hard* Bruce.

Hailey snapped her head around and practically hissed, "Did you find anything?" Then she cursed under her breath. I assumed she regretted having asked the question in my presence.

"No, just a bunch of old junk." He even pursed his lips like Bruce.

I spoke directly to Agent Die Hard. "One of the gentlemen assisting with the barn deconstruction told me it appeared this old barn had been used for just that purpose: a glorified junk drawer, if you will. They pretty much had it emptied out other than some odds and ends. The house and other outbuildings were torn down years ago. Thad, the young man who was working the wrecker, dragged the old Rambler from back there." I pointed inside the barn, scooped Riff into my arms, and strode into the darkness.

"Wait a minute, Mrs. Barrett; come back here," Hailey squealed most unprofessionally.

She minced up beside me, and Agent Die Hard followed, asking, "Where was the Rambler?"

Hailey did that Linda Blair–head rotation thing and glared. He pursed his lips shut and shifted his gaze between us in confusion.

In a clipped voice, she repeated the young man's question. "Where was the Rambler?"

I pointed to the far corner of the barn. "Over there, where the roof is starting to come down. Thad had to drag it out from under the debris." With a hand to Hailey's arm, I asked in concern, "Hailey, are you okay? Is this old barn spooking you? I can tell you're upset about something."

I detected a throaty snicker from Agent Die Hard before he moved toward the dark corner where I had pointed. Hailey called after him, "I'm taking Mrs. Barrett outside. It isn't safe in here." Hailey led the way through the large opening where only one door hung at a perilous angle.

I trotted behind, asking, "So, who was the man in the trunk? How long had he been in there? Is it too early in the autopsy to determine a cause of death?"

Hailey stopped to glare at me. Although her eye contact was no-nonsense, the smirk on her face made me want to slap it off. "I am unable to share any information with you, Mrs. Barrett. This is a TBI investigation; therefore, any information pertaining to the case can only be shared with trained law enforcement professionals."

*Nobody likes a smart-aleck TBI agent, Hailey*, I thought, but didn't say it.

Hailey broke the staring contest. "So, where is the tall to your short?"

"Come again?"

"Mrs. Honeycutt. The two of you are like lopsided bookends."

"Oh, Belinda broke her foot. She has to wear this awkward, clunky boot that pumps up like a bicycle tire. I left her home with her foot propped up on the sofa. She's sleeping off a pain pill."

"How did she break her foot?"

I started to weave another tangled web of deception, but Hailey interrupted irritably, "Never mind. I *don't* want to know."

Speaking of Belinda, my cell phone started to ring. I dropped Riff lightly to the ground and shoved the leash handle at Hailey. She accepted it out of reflex. I dug two-fisted into my purse. By the time I reached the phone, the ringing had stopped. The call log read: BELINDA.

Snatching the plastic handle back I sang, "Well, it was nice to see you again, Hailey. Good luck with your case." I hollered into the darkness of the barn, "Good-bye, Agent Huddleston," and made for my car.

"Mrs. Barrett," Hailey called, and I turned back. "Did you see anything in the trunk that could help with our investigation? Anything that looked out of place?"

I paused and screwed up my face as though I was giving the question great thought. "Well, now that you mention it, I never expected to find a dead, bony body inside the trunk of that old Rambler. Skeletons are outside the norm of trunk paraphernalia, although my sister used to haul around one or two skeletons in the trunk of her car on a regular basis. Margo wasn't a serial killer or anything. She sold school supplies.

She always had a spare skeleton in the trunk just in case a science class was in need of one."

I patted her hand. "I'm an old widowed lady, Hailey. You don't need my help. Good-bye, dear...and good luck."

Riff and I trotted toward the car. The grin on my face was pure evil.

I returned Belinda's call once I was behind the wheel. Belinda shrieked into the receiver, *"Leslie Barrett, get out of that old barn! You are going to get yourself killed!"*

"Calm down, Belinda. I'm not even in that old barn. Agent Donnelly is out here with a boy agent conducting an investigation. He's really cute; he looks a lot like Bruce Willis—you know, like Bruce looked in that *Die Hard* movie. Anyway, Tully's deconstruction job has been placed on hold for the duration. I'm on my way home now." I made more placating noises to my best friend and hung up.

# Chapter Eleven

When I got back to Belinda's, she met us at the front door on her secretary-skate-chair. "Leslie, I identified the key or at least I'm getting close. Why didn't you tell me about the key? Your note said you found it on the corpse, but we never saw the corpse, well, except for that skeletonized hand."

Riff and I trooped passed Belinda. As she rolled along behind us, I admitted, "Honestly, I forgot about the key until today when we were talking with Quinn. The first thing I saw in the trunk was that bony hand. Then I saw something shiny, and I picked it up. It was a key. It was lying on top of the quilt. That was when Thad swung me off my feet, and I dropped Riff's leash. She took off, and in all the excitement I stuck the key in my pocket."

"Uh-huh, sure. You expect me to believe that?"

"It's true! I forgot all about it. That lad is strong, by the way. He must have thought I was reaching for the quilt. What did you find out about the key? How are you feeling, by the way?"

"I feel okay; the nap helped a lot. I couldn't believe it when I read your note. I envisioned your broken body beneath the rubble of that ratty old barn." This was the scolding Belinda. *Not* my favorite Belinda.

"I couldn't just sit around. I had to do something. I thought maybe Tully and the guys were out there, and they could tell me more about the Madsen family. Instead, Miss Smart-aleck TBI Agent Hailey Donnelly was out there with her cute boy agent. Hailey said they have identified the body, but she wouldn't tell me anything: not his name, not how he died, not how long he had been stuffed in that trunk. Nothing. The woman is infuriating!"

"The boy agent wouldn't tell you anything?"

"No, Agent Die Hard was under the influence of Hailey. Hailey made it clear that she wasn't going to tell me anything."

I stomped into Belinda's kitchen and grabbed a Diet Coke from the fridge. Belinda took a seat at the kitchen table with her broken foot on the secretary chair. I waggled a Coke at her.

"No thanks, I'm kind of wired already. It didn't take me long to scope out that key on the Internet."

I sat across from her and took a satisfying gulp of the magic, caffeinated elixir. "So, what did you find out about the key?"

"First, I need to tell you that Mrs. Towers called—actually, the phone woke me up. Anyway, she spoke with Lilly about the Madsen family. Lilly confirmed Cecil Madsen was a successful banker who also leased acreage out for farming purposes. When old man Cecil died, the estate was split between his children. Lilly isn't a hundred percent positive, but she thinks there were only two. Oh yeah, according to Lilly, the funeral home *concierge* at Walton's is having an affair with one of his embalmers."

That last bit of gossip did not surprise me. I know firsthand what a roving eye that old codger has. At fat Marjorie Vickers' viewing, Mr. Funeral Home flirted with me shamelessly. I must have been secreting dark hormones that day. The old guy practically chased me down the hall.

I took another drink. "You know, Thad mentioned that his grandfather grew up with Denver Madsen. We should call him. Find out whether his grandfather is still around. Maybe he can tell us more about the family. Quinn said Thad's last name is Marshall and that his

family owns a boneyard. We need to look them up in the phone book."
I got up to grab her phone book.

"Leslie, while you're up, get the key. I left it beside my computer. Bring my notes too."

I returned with the key, her notes, and the phone book. I started to flip through the directory and then laid it aside. "We'll look up Marshall's family boneyard tomorrow. I'm tired. I didn't have a nap. Tell me what you found out about the key, and we'll regroup in the morning."

"I did an image search for old keys. I'm assuming that it's old; it looks old."

"Yeah, so did the skeleton. What did you come up with?"

"As you probably know, the only letters that can be made out are *T*, something, and two *R*s. Then—more scratched than engraved—the number forty-eight. I think it's some kind of railroad key. I don't know what kind of lock it's for, but it could be a key to something owned by the Tennessee Central Railway. You should get on the computer and read about it tonight. I'll keep searching too. I think this might be a critical clue. Did you tell Hailey Donnelly about the key?"

I snorted. "Heck no, if we are able to identify what kind of lock it goes to, maybe then we'll tell her. Maybe." I grinned at my friend. "Belinda, you're getting into this case, um, this situation. Usually, you don't encourage my curiosities."

"Looking into this *situation* is kind of fun. Whatever happened to the man in the trunk happened a very long time ago. It's a cold case. Looking into it is more of an intellectual pursuit than a dangerous one. You know, more of a puzzle than anything."

I quirked a grin. "Cold case? Have you been watching my cop shows?"

"Just *NCIS* and some reruns of *Murder, She Wrote*."

"You need to watch the CSI forensic-type shows. Jessica Fletcher was good, but she was old-school. She didn't have DNA and all that stuff. All she had were fingerprints and keen observations." I yawned. "I always thought it was stupid when the police picked up glasses and guns and stuff with a handkerchief. What if they were slapping that handkerchief smack over the only fingerprints on the thing? How many times did Jessica ask the cops about fingerprints, only to be told they couldn't identify the fingerprints because they were smudged?"

"I can't watch those grisly shows about autopsies, and stomach contents, and all that stuff."

"You're a nurse. I saw you standing there in front of that open trunk. I could practically hear your eyes clacking in your head."

"It's different when it's a real event. Objective clinical skills kick in. Just because I can handle the real thing doesn't mean I wish to fill my entertainment hours with body parts and stomach contents."

"I suppose. When I was twenty-one, I was a secretary for about thirty minutes. I hated it. When I told my boss I hated secretarial work, he said, 'But you have wonderful clerical skills.' I said I'm good at sex too, but I don't want to be a hooker. That shut him up. Then I quit."

I yawned again. "Riff and I are beat. We're going home. Why don't you take your rested self back to the Internet and see what else you can find out? I'll poke around too."

# Chapter Twelve

Just to prove to Mrs. Towers that I was capable of making dietary adjustments, I had a tuna salad sandwich and two glasses of water for dinner. Riff and I surfed—a high-tech term that means we looked stuff up—the Internet until 11:00 P.M. I found a lot of historical data about the Tennessee Central Railway. Up until today I'd never known we used to have a railroad in Clifton.

Contrary to Belinda's claim that I do not enjoy traveling, I might take a trip or two if I could travel by train. Air travel takes too long. Not the actual flight. I'm talking about simply getting on the plane. I get tired just thinking about all the waiting around. I long for the days when one could drive to an airport, present your appropriately purchased ticket, decline life insurance, get on a plane, and actually go somewhere. Oscar Meyer wieners take less processing than travelers today.

The idea of traveling by train is appealing, what with all the clacki-ty-clacking that goes on. Unfortunately, it's not as accessible as it used to be; I checked into it. Using Detroit as my destination, train travel would require either air or bus travel before even setting foot on an actual train. I would have to fly or take a bus to Memphis to catch the train. There isn't anyone I want to see badly enough to fool with every mode of transportation known to the human race. I want to get on a train where I want to get on and get off where I want to get off. Trains probably don't even clack anymore. Air travel is a nightmare and buses are—well, buses.

I haven't been reading good things about buses lately. They keep launching themselves off overpasses or pitching themselves into steep ravines. You don't hear about trains suddenly careening across the countryside… unless they contain flammable materials. I wouldn't board a train with flammable materials.

I like where I live. I don't need to travel.

According to the Internet, the Tennessee Central Railway came into being in the late 1800s for the primary purpose of moving coal. By the 1950s, the railway had pushed east of Nashville to wind its way through Middle Tennessee. The entire line was shut down in 1968. Allegedly, the old train depot in Clifton now houses a candy store called Clifton's Candy Depot. I don't recall seeing a Candy Depot in Clifton. It's a shame about the Tennessee Central having gone belly-up. It would have been convenient to catch a train leaving out of Clifton. I don't consider coal to be all that flammable. Coal is more of a simmering type of heat rather than the *whoosh-blooey* typical of petroleum products.

This was all fascinating, but I still didn't know what that stupid key was supposed to unlock. I decided to call it a night and wandered into the kitchen,  with Riff trailing. I picked up the phone book with the intention of finding an address and phone number for Marshall's boneyard. I couldn't find anything listed under boneyards so I looked in the sections covering automobiles or vehicles without success. I was ready to look under *junk* or *crap* when I spotted *junk dealers,* which led me to *scrap metal,* and finally…Marshall's Scrap Metal Recycling and Wrecker Service. I guess that sounded better to the Marshall clan than Marshall's Junkyard and Towing. I wrote down the information and left it by the phone. As Riff and I toddled off to bed, I was busily planning our activities for the following day. Belinda and I were making progress. I was convinced that the key would *unlock* the identity of the dead man in the trunk. I love to sharpen my mind on a good puzzle, and I was buoyed by Belinda's interest.

The next morning I was at Belinda's by 10:00 A.M. I didn't have to hang around in the bathroom anymore while she showered because she no longer booted up while at home now that she had the secretary-skate-chair. We drank coffee and discussed the Tennessee Central Railway.

"Belinda, the key has *T*, something, *R*, and *R*. *Tennessee Central Railroad*. What else could it be?"

"I don't know, but the *R R* part isn't accurate. The engraving should have been *R W* for *railway*, not *railroad*."

"It was a railroad. Maybe back then they thought *railway* sounded fancier, rather like the nursing home people referring to themselves as a living well center when everybody knows it's a nursing home. Even the people engraving the keys knew it was a railroad, hence, *R R* and not *R W*. This doesn't get us a whole lot closer to anything though. There must be a million things that key could have gone to on a railroad. A railroad that doesn't exist any longer." I like to use the word *hence*. *Hence* is a very smart word.

"What should we do next?"

"I suppose we could try calling Thad Marshall and see whether his grandfather is still around. Maybe grandpa can tell us more about the Madsen family. That might lead us somewhere. Maybe one of the Madsen boys went missing suddenly, or a farmhand." I smacked the table with the flat of my hand, "Darn that Hailey. Just knowing how long that guy was in that trunk would be a lead. If we knew that, we could look for the names of missing people and unsolved murders from that year. I looked at a bunch of them last night. There's one case in Tennessee that looked promising."

"Looked promising? What, somebody who went missing could be the man in the trunk?"

I nodded so vigorously, a sharp pain shot through my neck. "Yes, a radio dj in Chattanooga: Gus Tubman; his call name was the Gus Man. Tubman's car was discovered in 1971 on a lonely road south of Chattanooga. There was blood in the car but no Gus Tubman. His body was never found. The police thought that Gus might have been the victim of a hit man."

"A hit man? What was he doing, playing *bad* golden oldies? I imagine there are hundreds of cold cases in Tennessee. Why did you decide the man in the trunk is this Tubman person, and why would his killers haul him all the way from Chattanooga to Clifton?"

"I didn't say the man in the trunk is *definitely* Gus Tubman, Belinda. I'm alleging that the man *might* be Gus Tubman. I'm only using Gus as an example."

"It's unfortunate that poor Gus never turned up, but if Gus is your only candidate for the man in the trunk, we need to do a lot more research."

"Believe it or not, Elvis Presley's death is listed on one of those sites as suspicious."

Belinda gave me a get-out-of-town look. "Get out of town. Elvis' death in 1977 was due to natural causes, well, natural causes related to drug abuse, lifestyle, and what have you. Ultimately, I believe his death was a myocardial infarction, a heart attack."

"Like fat Marjorie Vickers?"

"Leslie, stop making fun of Marjorie's weight problem."

"I'm not making fun of Marjorie. Marjorie was fat, and she died of a heart attack. I'm simply making a comparison between her and Elvis Presley. Elvis getting fat like that was just wrong."

"Elvis died of a heart attack. It's ridiculous for Elvis to be on a website for suspicious deaths. You must have mixed up your websites."

"I did not. The site alleges that Elvis faked his own death, which is

idiotic. Why on Earth would Elvis fake his own death? It isn't like he
was a mobster or anything–Frank Sinatra, maybe, but not Elvis."

"That's ludicrous! I'm seeing a pattern developing here, Les. Evidently
you want the man in the trunk of your Nash Rambler to be a rock and
roller. So far our choices are Gus Tubman or Elvis Presley."

"No, no, no. I was merely looking at mysterious deaths, and missing
men in Tennessee starting in the 1950s. The Rambler was manufac-
tured in the fifties. Gus wasn't a rock and roller. He simply played rock
and roll on the radio." My eyes filled with nostalgic tears. "Remember
Elvis in the 1968 comeback TV special, Belinda? All that black hair,
those eyes, and the tight black leather—the man was gorgeous! After
that he went to Las Vegas, got fat, and died. Poor Elvis, but man, he
looked *good* in sixty-eight."

Belinda heaved a mighty sigh. "He did; he surely did."

Sadly, we agreed Elvis was probably dead, and I placed a call to
Marshall's Scrap and Whatever and asked for Thad.

"Hey, Mrs. Barrett. Tully's crew isn't working today; those TBI people
have the Madsen barn site locked down."

"I know, Thad. You mentioned that your grandfather grew up with
one of old Mr. Madsen's sons, didn't you?"

"Yeah, Granddaddy says he used to hang out hunting and fishing
with old Cecil's boy Denver. Why do you ask?"

"So, your grandfather is still alive?"

"Oh, sure. Granddaddy is close to seventy, but he's in pretty good
health. What's this about, Mrs. B?"

"Seventy isn't old, Thad. What do they say nowadays: seventy is the
new forty or some such nonsense." That close-to-seventy comment
didn't set well with me.

"Not in my granddaddy's case. He's got two bad knees, high-blood
pressure, and can't hear a Fourth of July parade. Mama had to get him

one of those loud-talking telephones."

I gave up on the close-to-seventy jab and started babbling instead. "We'd like to talk to your grandfather. Mrs. Honeycutt and I are curious about the identity of the man in the trunk and how he might have wound up in that trunk."

"Oh, I get it. You're looking into the mystery of the guy in the trunk the way you did when that old guy was fished out of Lake Manchester! I heard you got into something over at the cemetery too."

I nodded, but he couldn't see me through the phone so I said, "Yes, Thad, like we did with our friend Abner Cummings and the rest of it." I held my breath, hoping he wouldn't tell me to take up knitting or something. Thad didn't disappoint.

"You want to talk to my granddaddy? No problem. The senior citizens' bus drops Granddaddy off at the junkyard at three o'clock. He hangs out here with the dogs and me until I get off at five. Then he rides home with me. We have a system. Works real well too. Why don't you ladies swing by today? I know Granddaddy will be tickled to help you with your dead-body mystery."

We made arrangements to swing by the junkyard after our visit to the nursing home.

# Chapter Thirteen

I reluctantly turned my dog over to the nursing home receptionist on the way in. Riff didn't seem to mind. She got a lot of attention, and choruses of "Oh, what a cute dog" followed us down the hallway.

We turned the corner into the rehab wing and were elated to see Mrs. Towers in the hallway on her walker with one of the PT staff whose name tag read MISSY. Mrs. Towers waved with a big grin.

"She looks great!" Belinda said, then added in a hushed voice, "Uh-oh, purse lady at six o'clock."

I swung around to greet Mrs. Turley and was ready when she asked, "Have you ladies seen Mitch Turley?"

"Not today, Mrs. Turley," I admitted.

Mrs. Turley glanced at Belinda's boot. "What happened to your foot?"

I launched into a colorful story about how my friend had been water skiing in Florida, took one of those jump ramps, and slammed into the water, breaking the skis and her foot.

"Oh," she said before turning on her heel.

Belinda chuckled. "Water skiing?"

"Why not. You should live a little, take a few chances."

We waited around until Mrs. Towers had completed her PT session. "How's she doing?" I asked Missy.

"Great, just great. We just needed to get her out of that bed."

We talked for a couple of minutes, then the young woman left us standing beside Mrs. Towers, now seated on her bed with her legs dangling over the side.

"They started getting me up after the two of you left yesterday. You heard Missy, I'm doing great. I want to go home. I asked the nurse to call the doctor and get a discharge order. She refused to make the call. Can you imagine? Has the Italian lady moved in yet?"

Did the nurse say why she refused to call the doctor?" I asked, and added, "No, according to Lenore, she's moving in sometime next week. She's still waiting for the paperwork."

"Good. Hopefully, I'll be home before her then. The nurse sent that little witch of a social worker in here. *Karen* said she had spoken with Valerie, and Valerie agreed it was too soon for me to go home. I called Valerie and told her I was writing her out of the will."

"What did she have to say to that?" Belinda snickered.

"I left a message on the machine. The coward hasn't returned my call. They can't keep me here. This is kidnapping!" Eyes filling with tears, she sniffled, "I want to go home. I'm doing great, and I want to go home."

"No one can make you stay here, Mrs. Towers, but if your doctor feels you're not ready to go home, that should be his call."

"It's nobody's call except mine." She huffed.

I nodded. "That's true. If your doctor disagrees with you, you have the right to sign yourself out against medical advice. However, once assured you have adequate support at home, I don't believe your doctor will refuse to give a discharge order."

"What kind of support?"

Belinda's nurse training kicked in. "You can get PT at home through a home health agency. After watching you today, you look like you're regaining your strength. You still need to work on your stamina though."

Mrs. Towers was about to object, but Belinda held her off with a hand. "There are a few changes you need to make at home to ensure you're safe, and to help you regain your strength and stamina."

"Like what? You just said I can get PT at home."

I began my social worker spiel. "Like, for example, you need to keep your help-gizmo with you at all times. You don't have to wear it around your neck, but perhaps you could attach it to your walker somehow. You go off without your help-gizmo all the time, but you never go anywhere without your walker. And we need to declutter your place. You shouldn't be maneuvering around all those stupid little tables and knickknacks."

"Leslie, everything I display in my home means a great deal to me."

"Fine. I can accept that, but we can line them up somewhere rather than have them scattered all over the place."

She threw me such a sad look that I hurried to clarify, "Look, we all have to make adjustments as we get older. I have been standing on my bed to dust the ceiling fan in my bedroom for years. The other day I climbed up there and started seesawing back and forth as if I were in a rowboat. I caught a look at myself in the mirror above the bureau and had to laugh at the sight. I looked ridiculous waving that yellow Swiffer around."

Mrs. Towers laughed, and Belinda strangled on a snicker.

I took a risk. "Another valuable service, while living alone and recuperating, is to arrange for Meals on Wheels."

"Oh, Leslie, no." Mrs. Towers yelped in horror. "I promise I will line up my knickknacks like soldiers next to the walls, I will carry my help-gizmo with me everywhere, and I will not jump on the bed; just don't force me to get Meals on Wheels!"

Belinda contributed a nugget of sheer genius. "I know, we can get you protein drinks. They taste really good. Leslie is right. If you don't take better care of yourself, you're going to be right back where you started."

"Yeah, sitting all alone in an empty garage searching for Abner Cummings, who, by the way, is dead." I huffed dramatically.

Mrs. Towers smirked. "Ha! You said I had Riff with me. I wasn't alone."

Mrs. Towers agreed to postpone any demands for immediate release—"But I'm going home tomorrow. I don't care what anyone says." As we headed to the door, she called after us, "Hey, if you get me those protein drinks, get chocolate."

As we returned to the lobby, Belinda said, "She means it, Leslie."

"I know; Mrs. Towers loves chocolate."

She punched me playfully on the arm as we walked. "You know what I mean."

"Yes, we'll deal with it tomorrow."

We had some time to kill until three o'clock., so we stopped by a Dollar General Store. We were taking a big risk; this wasn't *our* Dollar General. We puttered around for a while until a lady wearing a store badge approached to inform me that pets were not allowed. I went into my huffing-and-puffing rant until she gave up and walked away. What's the big deal about having an eight-or-so-pound dog in my cart? We aren't talking about some big galoot of a dog. Riff isn't a Great Dane. She's not going to go crazy and mow down half the store. Riff couldn't knock over anything more substantial than a roll of paper towels.

I like to paw through the clearance stuff. I rarely find anything of interest, but I like to paw anyway. Today it paid off. "Hey, Belinda, look at this!" I held up a small plastic pocket thing with a Velcro strap attached to it.

Coming in for a closer look she frowned. "What is it?"

"I have no idea. What I'm thinking though is that Mrs. Towers can strap this pocket thing to the handle of her walker."

"For what, her sidearm?"

"Ha-ha, no, for her help-gizmo." I grinned, proud of my ingenuity.

Taking the pocket thing in her hand, she turned it over. "This is probably intended to hold a cell phone, but it should work just as well for Mrs. Towers' help-gizmo. Good job, Leslie!"

I swear, turn me loose in a Dollar General Store, and I can find anything.

# Chapter Fourteen

Marshall's Scrap Metal and Junkyard Towing (or whatever) was a fascinating place. For a junkyard, it was very organized. Dollar General is junkier than this place. I drove through the gates and headed toward a small building with a sign on it that said OFFICE. "That must be the office, Belinda."

"Ya think?"

I ignored the sarcasm and hurried around the rear of the Soul to meet Belinda climbing from the passenger seat. With Riff tucked under one arm, I waved in the direction of a crane. A gigantic magnet dangled from a bunch of thick chains and cables. "Look at that contraption. You could bring your church ladies out here. I wouldn't bring Maria Tuff though. With all those replacement knees and hips, she's liable to find herself swinging from that magnet next to a 1973 Ford Pinto."

Belinda offered a humorless smile. We were startled by a beaming giant of a man who threw open the office door and with arms wide boomed, "Welcome to Sanford and Son's," followed by a fit of laughter, followed by a fit of coughing.

As we entered, Thad waved from a desk off to the side and covered the phone mouthpiece. "Granddaddy, keep it down. I'm on the phone. Hey, ladies, this is my Granddaddy Raymond." He returned to his phone conversation.

Belinda stepped forward and began introductions. "Mr. Marshall, we appreciate you taking the time to talk with us. I'm Belinda Honeycutt, and this is my friend Leslie Barrett. We were at the old Madsen place yesterday."

*"CAN'T HEAR YA, MA'AM. SPEAK UP!"*

Thad glanced over and hollered, *"GRANDDADDY, PUT IN YOUR HEARING AIDS."*

*"OH...JUST A SECOND."* Granddaddy Raymond patted his pockets and then screwed a hearing aid into each ear. He fiddled and tuned them for a bit and then said with a grin, "Sorry about that. These confounded things honk and squeal so much that sometimes it isn't worth using them. Now, what were those names again? I sure hope you two ladies aren't married. My little black book could use a couple of lookers like you."

Belinda has a talent. She can go all girly, flirty, coy with just a tilt of her head. She repeated the introductions, albeit with a wily feminine bend.

"Name is Raymond Turner, but you can call me Ray. My Thelma married Thad's daddy. Stu Marshall is a fine son-in-law. Yup, Thelma got lucky when she married that one. Thad over here is a pretty good ole boy hisself. Come in, ladies, and have a sit-down."

Ray Turner was easily six-five and well fed. His thinning hair was buzzed so close to his head I could almost count the freckles on his scalp. Hanging up the phone, Thad grinned at the compliment. "Granddaddy, these are the two ladies I told you about; they're the ones who figured out what happened to that old guy in Lake Manchester last summer. Now they're looking into what happened to that man we found in the car trunk the other day, maybe find out who the fella was. You said that you grew up with Denver Madsen, so I thought perhaps you could help them with their investigation."

With a wide grin full of blindingly white dentures, Ray Turner repeated the laughing/coughing routine. "Boy, now that was something.

You two out there in the Glen solving the mystery of the turtle man." He squinted eyes at Riff. "Is that a *dog* you got there, Miss B? You wanna see our guard dogs? We got these two big dogs to protect the junkyard at night. Want to see 'em?"

Thad cautioned, "Granddaddy…"

Belinda and I tossed frightened looks back and forth as I sputtered, "No, no, really, Raymond, er, Ray. No, thank you."

Ignoring my plea the old man bellowed toward the back, "Hey, Marv, let our two girls out to meet these ladies!"

A door at the end of a hallway opened, and I heard the scrabble of dog toenails against the linoleum. We let out girly squeals of fright expecting two slobbering, junkyard dogs to appear. Instinctively, I clutched Riff with both hands and pointed her toward the ceiling in an attempt to keep my fur ball from the mouths of the ferocious beasts. Belinda plucked Riff from my hands and held her even higher. I gave a furtive glance toward the ceiling. I am cautious about Belinda's height and ceiling fans. Fortunately, Riff wasn't in imminent danger of an unscheduled grooming. She had plenty of clearance, and the fan wasn't on anyway.

Two beautiful greyhounds pranced into the room, as sleek and elegant as runway models. One was the color of sand and the other, a smoky gray. They stopped as they entered the room and looked at Ray as though seeking permission to enter.

"Sorry if I scared you, ladies. It's a little trick I like to pull on folks. The sandy one is Cyd, and the gray one is Charisse. Cyd, Charisse, say hello to the ladies and that little, white, fluffy mess that's maybe one of them guinea pigs."

The dogs approached cautiously, their tails whipping fiercely back and forth on hearing our squeals of delight. Riff twisted and wriggled in Belinda's hands until Belinda tentatively set her on the floor, not fully releasing her from her grasp. Cyd and Charisse danced over to sniff the little visitor. Once we were sure all was safe, Belinda released Riff, and the three new friends proceeded to become acquainted in typical doggy style, that is, by sniffing butts.

"This is my dog, Riff-Raff; she's a Maltese-and-something-else."

Soon the animals were sprawled in a tangle on the floor. Belinda fluttered at Ray, "I love their names! Cyd and Charisse, because of those long, shapely legs,   I'll bet."

Ray and Thad went on to tell us about having adopted the dogs from the National Greyhound Adoption Program.

Belinda and I took our seats, after which Ray lowered his grateful bulk into a rocking chair and launched into his story.

"Old Cecil Madsen made his money in banking, and by leasing his land to others for farming—you know, sharecropping, sort of. Cecil was a mean, stingy old man. He and Barbara had two kids: Denver, who was my age, and Marcella, who was eight years younger. I think little Marcy was a surprise baby. She was a pretty little thing. When we was growing up, Denver watched over her like she was a baby chick. Denver died a little over a year ago and left the properties to his son, Fred. Denver held out on selling to the Fairlawn Glen people for some reason that none of us could figure."

I leaned into the conversation. "I understand Denver had the main house and outbuildings destroyed but left the old barn intact. What happened to his sister?  She didn't inherit?"

"The way I remember it, Denver got the properties, and Marcy got a bunch of money. Marcy's got COPD real bad. You know what that is?"

Belinda answered, "Yes. Chronic obstructive pulmonary disease. It's not uncommon in heavy smokers; of course, there are other causes."

"Marcy got hers the old-fashioned way. Been sucking on those cancer sticks since she was twelve."

"Where is Marcy now?" I asked.

"She married Lou Scrimger and had some kids. I recall reading that Lou died in some kind of freak farming accident a long time ago. The last I heard, Marcy was living over there in that Clifton nursing home place. You know, it's got some goofy name, *The Living Will* or somethin'. From what I hear the poor woman can't take but a few steps without sucking on that oxygen tube like it was a tit."

Thad warned, "Granddaddy..."

"Sorry, ladies. Marcy must be around sixty-three, way too young to be stuck in some nursing home. Reckon she can't blame anybody 'cept herself. I chucked cigarettes forty years ago. Otherwise I'd likely be six feet under by now."

"What were the Madsen kids like?"

"Denver was a good, solid fella. Like I said, he looked after his little sister like she was something precious. Marcy had a bit of a wild streak in her as a teenager. Got herself a bit of a reputation, but Denver would whip anybody who cracked jokes about her."

"Do you have any idea who that man in the car trunk could be? Do you recall anyone going missing who knew the Madsen family or lived or worked on their properties maybe, like a farmhand or sharecropper, that sort of thing?" I pressed.

He thought for a long time, then lifted a trembling finger. "I do recall one young fella. He was around our age, Denver and me, I mean. His name was...Oh, dammit, what was that boy's name?"

"Let it roll around in your head for a bit, Granddaddy. It'll come to you later."

Belinda leaned forward. "Ray, what can you tell us about the Tennessee Central Railway?"

"The old railroad? That was a big deal there for about twenty years or so, back in the fifties and sixties. Was supposed to haul coal and be a real moneymaker. The moneymaking never seemed to pan out though. Poor management or squabbling owners or somethin'. They shut the whole mess down in the late sixties or early seventies. I don't think there's much left anymore, just that little bit of track that the locomotive sets on down there by the old depot. I hear they turned the station into a candy store—kept the depot intact as a historical place. Why, what does the old railroad have to do with anything?"

"Maybe nothing…" I was trying to make up something when Ray interrupted with a shout. "Warren somebody! That was that fella's name who just disappeared when Denver and I were around twenty-three or so. He was a troublemaker. There one day and just gone the next. The rumor was that he went and got killed in Vietnam. I remember him because Denver was always warning him to stay clear of his little sister; then again, Denver told me to stay clear of his little sister, so it may not mean much."

"What year do you think this Warren somebody took off? You said he was around the same age as you and Denver, and that the two of you were around twenty-three?"

Ray's eyes were wide as he rocked back in his chair. "Do you think the man in the trunk is Warren? Wow, wouldn't that be something." He closed his eyes tightly and on opening them said, "Me and Denver, that would have been around 1968. Does that help?"

"It would if anyone reported Warren as missing. Did he have any family that you recall? Did he work anywhere, the railroad perhaps?"

Ray resumed rocking and thinking with a hand on Cyd's neck. "I don't think Warren had anybody. He stayed off and on with some of the other guys, but I don't remember him having any family. That's why we all didn't question the rumor about him joining the army. Warren was one of those fringe kind of people. He never belonged to anyone. He didn't have nothing to do with the railroad as far as I recollect. The rest of us boys did farmwork and such until Denver went to work in one of his daddy's banks. Warren didn't seem to do much of anything."

Turning toward Thad, I asked, "Did you get a look at what was under that quilt after Belinda and I left?"

With a gulp, he admitted, "Well, I stood off to the side, just like I was told, but when Chief Braddock lifted the quilt, I sort of peeked. All I saw was a tangle of long black hairs, then I couldn't look any longer."

I snapped, "Quinn lifted the quilt? I'm surprised he would compromise evidence like that."

"Oh, he poked it up with a stick. He never touched anything," he rushed to clarify.

I glared at Belinda. "Did you hear that? Quinn lifted it with a stick."

"Yes, Leslie. I heard."

Then the conversation segued into more mundane topics such as how Ray still has a truck but doesn't do much driving anymore because of his bad leg. He needs a knee replacement but keeps putting it off. Anyway, when people start talking about their aches and pains that no one really cares about, I start looking for alternative entertainment. I found myself across the room with the dogs. Sitting cross-legged on the floor, I was petting the two greyhound beauties until Riff objected and scrambled onto my lap.

"Okay, Riff," I mumbled, and started the process of standing up with Riff tucked under one arm. "Uh-oh." When no one rushed to my aid, I called a little louder, "*UH-OH!*"

Belinda snickered, "She's down, and she can't get up."

Thad leaped from his chair like a sheriff in an old Western and galloped across the room. I assisted as much as I could by grunting. There are a lot of dumb scientific studies funded by the government. A good one might be to determine at what age loud vocalization enhances body mechanics. *I* started groaning like a lawn mower in my forties.

We thanked Ray and Thad for the information about the Madsen family. Petting Cyd and Charisse in farewell—the considerate animals stood to hand-petting level—I asked Ray, "These two long-legged beauties don't actually patrol the junkyard, do they?"

Ray laughed the same booming laugh we'd heard on entering. "No way! Thad and his daddy have one of those security systems with cameras and everything. These ladies are just for loving on; they don't have to work no more. I sure wish I could've helped you ladies figger out who that fella was in that trunk."

"We do too," I commiserated. "Hopefully, the TBI will be able to find some forensic evidence in that Rambler. It may take them a while to process everything."

"Didn't take long at all; Quinn called the very next day to ask me to come to the Safety Department and haul it off. He said the TBI people had finished with it."

My jaw dropped. "You mean to tell me they released the car after only one day?"

"Yes, ma'am."

"And, you brought it back here?"

"Yes, ma'am. Had to load it on the rollback on account of the rotted tires. Couldn't drag it behind a wrecker on naked rims."

"Where is it now? You didn't haul it up with the gigantic magnet out there and smoosh it into an itty-bitty cube, did you?"

"Oh no, ma'am. Believe it or not, there are still some parts on that old heap that people would buy."

"No one will buy that rusted old mess."

"Parts. There are lots of people that restore those old cars. Vintage parts can be fixed up. Folks will post on the Internet that they are looking for part so-and-so to go on, for example, a Rambler from the 1950s. You'd be surprised."

Belinda was already outside the office and turned back. "I can see that, Les. It would be like building a Frankenstein monster. I can't imagine any part of that car being valuable though."

"Heck, I had a fella pay me a hundred dollars for the trunk of a 1965 Ford Falcon. He was restoring one out in Baton Rouge, Louisiana. The old heap he bought didn't have a trunk floor any longer. It had rusted out from water damage after it was left in an old barn. Lots of those old cars turn up in barns. Just like the Rambler did."

"Can we look in the trunk of the Rambler again?" I asked excitedly.

Old killjoy Belinda warned, "Leslie, the TBI have already gone over that trunk. Looking in the trunk isn't going to do any good."

"It isn't going to do any harm either." I shook her off. "How about it, Thad? Can I look in the trunk?"

"Sure, the car's right around back here."

We hopped down the stairs, and I followed him around the building. Belinda trailed us, grumbling under her breath. The Rambler was still on the bed of the rollback. I stood staring up at it. "How do you get up there?"

"We have a hydraulic lift that lowers the bed of the truck and rolls it back so we can winch the car onto the bed. Want me to roll it back?"

"No. I think I can climb up there. Loud machinery scares me to death. I like to watch machines, but I don't want to be in the middle of one, if you know what I mean." I handed Riff over to Belinda. "Take Riff, please."

"Les, don't try to climb up there," she pleaded.

"I'll be all right." I was glad I had worn my green Levis and matching Keds–perfect for climbing around on trucks.

"Here, Mrs. B, let me lift you up there and I'll climb up after you."

Before I even had time to consider the offer, two strong hands gripped my waist and up in the air I went. I found myself sitting on the edge

of the bed. I was surprised he had managed the maneuver so effort-
lessly and quickly. I was a bit breathless and speechless. Thad seemed
to be manhandling me on a regular basis. I found his youthful strength
impressive and invigorating, to say the least. He hopped up onto the
truck bed and lifted me to my feet in seconds.

I walked around the Rambler in my quiet Keds, with Thad clomping
behind in work boots. "You really believe there are parts of this thing
that you can sell?"

"Sure, even that knob on the tip of the gearshift. It could be just the
piece someone is searching for. Or the radio. Not the guts of the radio–
those are long gone–but the radio housing itself. Those parts may not
look like much, but if you cleaned them up some, they're almost as
good as new."

We had circled the car to the trunk. "Can you open it?"

He whipped a screwdriver from a back pocket. "No problem. The
lock is busted anyway." The metal squealed and popped as he opened
it. "I'll hold it up for you."

I leaned into the trunk and pointed. "Look, do you see that scrap of
fabric way back in there?"

He craned his neck to peer beneath his arm. "Yeah, it's blue. You
reckon it's a piece of that quilt? Can't imagine the TBI people over-
looked it."

I snorted with derision. "I'm afraid Hailey isn't the most capable
agent in Tennessee."

"Hailey had the rest of the quilt to examine, Les," Belinda pointed
out in her let's-be-reasonable Belinda voice.

"She doesn't have that blue piece, now does she?" I retorted airily.

"Obviously the TBI got what they needed. There isn't any reason for
you to go climbing around in there. You'll get all scraped up and dirty.
Who knows what kind of critters have been living in there."

She had a point. Especially about mice trails and such. I looked longingly at the trunk. "I'd really like to get my hands on that material."

Thad looked over at Belinda, who was watching from the side of the truck with Riff in her arms. "Mrs. H, how about you go back inside the office and ask Granddaddy to give you some sheets of plastic. It's new stuff. We can put it on the edge of the bumper so Mrs. B can climb over it and reach that fabric. Unless you want to get up here and hold up this trunk lid. Then I can reach in there and snag it."

"Let Leslie hold the trunk open for you."

"She's too short. She can't hold the lid up high enough."

Belinda sighed loudly and turned. "I'll get the plastic."

She was back in a few minutes minus Riff. She had an armload of plastic sheeting and handed it up to me. "I left Riff inside with Ray and the girls. Leslie, you be careful."

I held up the trunk lid while Thad folded several layers of plastic over the rusted-out back bumper. Then he set a couple of sheets inside the trunk. "Lay this sheeting down in front of you, Mrs. B. You sure you don't want me to try?"

"Take the trunk lid, Thad. I found that poor man's body. I have a connection with him. I feel I owe it to him to thoroughly investigate."

Thad stiff-armed the trunk, and I threw my left leg over the plastic.

Belinda oozed derision. "Good grief, Les. Could you be any more dramatic?!"

"Shut up," I sniffed, climbing fully into the trunk to sit in a crouch on my butt. The trunk space was dinky. There was a round indentation in the floor with one rod sticking up in the middle. I laid my hand on the rim. "This must be where the spare tire was stored."

Thad nodded professionally. "More 'n likely."

"Les, get that scrap and get out of there."

I wanted to narrow my eyes at my friend, but I couldn't turn around in the trunk enough to meet her eyes. So I ignored her instead. I stretched into the trunk on my left side with my left leg jackknifed beneath me. I pointed the toes on my right foot as though the effort would elongate my body. The fabric was caught under the lip where the used-to-be-red-painted metal met the rotted out trunk lining. I worked it free, transferred it to my right hand, and gave it to Thad. "Take this," I grunted, my voice sounded strained and muffled by the trunk, as well as my physical efforts. My left knee was starting to hurt, but I'd rather die than admit it. I bent at the waist to maneuver my head over the well where a spare tire used to live. I felt Thad's hand cover the top of my head to protect it from hitting the trunk lid. I giggled. "That's what the cops do when they secure a crook in the backseat of a patrol car."

He chuckled. "Give me your hands."

I turned my head to look at him. "But you won't be able to hold the lid if…" My eyes met Belinda's. The hand protecting my head belonged to my best friend in the entire world. "Belinda," I grunted, "when did you…"

Thad cut me off. "Mrs. H, hold up the lid while I lift her out of there."

Belinda straightened up and held the trunk lid high. Thad leaned into the trunk. I reached out with my right hand and clasped it in his. He started to tug. My head was still hovering above the tire well when I saw something. "Wait, stop a minute."

He released my hand, and I leaned closer to the empty tire well. "There's something down there." My left hand rested on top of the plastic, and I reached my right arm into the empty well.

"Gawd, Les, don't do that. Don't touch anything in there." Belinda sounded almost scared.

"I need to see what's down there."

"You've practically got your head down in that hole."

"So what?"

"Leslie, just look how you have to scrunch up just to fit in there."

"So?"

"So, that man's body was crammed in there, that's what's so. You saw that skeletonized hand lying on that trunk lining. There wasn't anything between the floor of that trunk and that man's body."

"So?"

"Okay, fine…I'll just say it. That body wasn't always a skeleton, Leslie!" She lowered her voice when she saw my eyes widen in understanding. "You're the one who loves to watch all those disgusting forensic shows on TV. When the human body decomposes…"

I started to shake. "*Why* are you just now telling me this?"

"I told you not to climb in there."

I started to breathe out as though I was giving birth. "*Phoo…phoo… phoo…*"

Thad reached for me. "C'mon, give me your hands."

I flapped my right hand at him. "No. I'm okay. I'm in here now. I'm going to see what's down here." I leaned into the well again to look. "It's a piece of plastic."

"Just leave it," Belinda ordered.

"Wait. There's something inside." I plucked the plastic thing from where it had been wedged beneath what must have been a tire jack or something. Cupping it in my palm, I shouted excitedly into the tire well, "It's a coin!"

Belinda was becoming interested now. "A coin?"

"I wonder if there are any more of them in this trunk?" I said hollowly into the tire well.

"Give it to Thad and get out of there, Les."

I straightened and yelped at the pain in my hip and knee.

I slapped the plastic something into Thad's hand, and he laid it on the truck bed before lifting me from the trunk as though he were carrying me over a threshold.

I kept up a litany of "*Ow...ow...ow...ow...*" until he allowed my legs to drop and my feet met the floor of the flatbed.

"Stand back," Belinda ordered. "I'm releasing the trunk lid."

She let it go, and we all jumped back. Instead of a hearty *BAM*, it smacked into the wadded-up plastic and settled with a muffled *FWAP*.

With one hand on my back, I stretched in an attempt to get out the kinks. Thad jumped from the truck bed. Belinda helped me sit on the edge so Thad could set me on the ground. Then she allowed Thad to put her on the ground as well.

I was flexing my left leg back and forth and then jogging in place. Belinda held out a coin in the palm of her hand. "It's a fifty-cent piece. Kennedy, 1964. It looks perfect."

"Wow. I wonder how much it's worth."

"Fifty cents," Thad muttered, causing us both to look at him. He was examining the scrap of fabric. Noticing us, he added, "Oh, I mean I don't know." He held the material out for us to see. "Look, there's part of a poodle."

I insisted the scrap be placed in a plastic bag to protect any forensic evidence. I scolded Belinda for having removed the coin from its plastic sleeve but not before I had smothered the coin in my own fingerprints. Nevertheless, we returned the coin to its sleeve and then secured both in their own plastic bag. "We'll notify the TBI that we handled the coin and plastic sleeve. Otherwise, Hailey Donnelly will charge both of us with murder."

"Les, that coin probably has nothing to do with the man's murder, assuming it was murder."

"It was murder. We've already had this conversation."

Ray had been thrilled with the discoveries and ran around like a kid to produce a box of sandwich-size Ziploc bags.

We went through our whole good-bye routine again and headed to the car, our forensic evidence tucked away inside Belinda's purse. I stood on my tiptoes to glare at Belinda over the roof of the Soul. Fisting my bangs in emphasis, I said, "Did you hear what Thad said, Belinda? The man in the trunk had long, black hair. Elvis had long, black hair."

Shaking her head dismissively, she returned my glare. "Elvis didn't have long, straggly hair."

Once we were inside the car I handed Riff off to her. She fastened her seat belt in place and continued in her preachy Belinda voice, "The man in the trunk is *not* Elvis. The next time you see Regina, tell her to cut your bangs. You're driving me crazy grabbing at them all the time."

"Yeah, I know, they're making me crazy too, but listen to this, just hear me out. Elvis Presley had all that beautiful blue-black hair, maybe the hair Thad saw only looked long because, well, the head shrivels all up after…"

"I know all about the postmortem shriveling process of the human body. As you will recall, I tried to warn you about climbing into that nasty trunk. I thought we agreed Elvis died of a heart attack. And that Gus person's car was way over by Chattanooga. You know that."

I scraped my bangs from my face again. "Just listen. What if…" I plowed right through Belinda's scowl. "What if Elvis actually died after that TV special in 1968. I have no idea why he would have been hanging around the Clifton area, but just supposing he was."

"Leslie…"

"At least do me the courtesy of hearing me out," I whined.

She settled back in the passenger seat, stroking Riff's fur. "Fine. I'll listen, but you're being ridiculous."

"Now, suppose somebody murdered Elvis back then when the man looked good enough to swallow whole, and then somebody went to

Las Vegas pretending to be Elvis, and that was the big fat guy who died in 1977!"

When I finished, Belinda clucked her tongue. "And I suppose the mysterious railroad key and the pristine Kennedy half-dollar belonged to Elvis's murderer, and the murderer hopped a train to Las Vegas, where he perfected his impersonation of Elvis? Leslie, I hate it that Elvis let himself get all fat like that too, but what you're suggesting is a nutty conspiracy theory. You really need to stop watching Fox News."

# Chapter Fifteen

We played around a little that evening on the Internet trying to match the key to a lock but didn't get anywhere. While we were at it, I showed Belinda that Elvis Presley's death *is* listed as suspicious on a Tennessee site. I can't help it. I prefer my conspiracy theory to the reality that Elvis really did get fat. Belinda wouldn't consider the possibility. "The man in our trunk is not Elvis Presley. Wanting him to be that svelte, sexy, 1968 man is not going to make it so."

We kept seeing these big padlocks called switch locks and keys, but that didn't make any sense. We couldn't fathom why the man in the trunk would be carrying around a key that shifts one railroad rail to another unless he worked on the railroad. An average guy would have no reason to run around switching rails. It isn't as though he'd happen to come across some railroad men struggling to switch rails and leap to their aid brandishing a rail-switching key. Ray said he wasn't aware of any of the guys working on the railroad back in 1968. We also conducted a search of valuable old coins. A pristine 1964 Kennedy half-dollar is now worth around ten dollars due to the silver content more than anything else. Starting in 1965 the percentage of silver in the half-dollar was reduced from 90 percent to 40 percent. Although this information was interesting, the existence of the sleeved coin didn't shed any light on the overall mystery of the dead man in the trunk. The coin could have been wedged in that tire well since 1964 since our search also revealed that people started hoarding the Kennedy half-dollar immediately on its release in 1964. The finding of the coin—although mysterious—didn't bring us any closer to solving the murder mystery.

Belinda, Riff, and I were headed back out to the nursing home at eleven the next morning. Belinda waved at our soon-to-be-new Italian neighbor, who stood beside the real estate agent while she unlocked the front door. The attractive woman returned the wave. Belinda sighed. "Abner would have approved."

I chuckled and fluffed my hair. "Hey, we aren't chopped liver."

"You are!" She laughed. "Regina is going to have a fit when she sees the crooked mess you made of your bangs. You and a pair of scissors should never be in close proximity to each other."

I had indeed chopped my bangs the night before. "I don't care. It's my hair. It's your fault anyway. You kept harping about my bangs." I glanced from the rearview mirror to Belinda. "I think we're being followed."

She swung around in her seat to look and whacked her booted foot on the car door. "*Ow!* What are you talking about?"

"Back there." I motioned with my head. "There's an old green truck back there. It was parked off to the side and fell in behind us as we drove through the gates. Then it followed us on to Trendle Road."

"So what? There's only one way into town. If you go to town from the Glen, you're going to turn on to Trendle."

"I'm keeping an eye on that truck," I muttered darkly.

I could hear the eye roll in her voice. "Here we go again. Can you tell whether Elvis is driving?"

"You don't have to be so sarcastic. I agreed Elvis is dead. All I suggested was that the big, fat guy who died in 1977 was not the *real* Elvis Presley. I merely alleged that Elvis was bumped off after the 1968 TV special. The murderer assumed his identity and went on to star in

Las Vegas, got fat, and died. There's a whole bunch of people out there who agree with me."

I inherited my suspicious nature from my mother. Mom was convinced that mobsters followed her everywhere, which was silly; everybody knew all the mobsters were in Chicago. Nobody ever heard of mobsters in Flint, Michigan. Union thugs maybe, but the Chicago-style mobsters my mother hallucinated everywhere in Flint were in Chicago.

I thought I saw the truck two more times before we pulled off for the nursing home. Then, I forgot about it. While the receptionist cooed over Riff, I asked, "Do you know whether Marcella Madsen lives out here? She's an old friend of ours. We wanted to drop by before we visit Mrs. Towers."

"No, ma'am, I don't recognize the name."

"Belinda, who did Marcy Madsen marry? I can't remember Lou's last name." Belinda and I had worked out this routine in advance.

"Scrimger. Marcy married Lou Scrimger."

The little receptionist was bobbing her head up and down happily. "Marcy Scrimger... sure, Mrs. Scrimger resides in our assisted living wing." She clicked the keys in front of her and announced, "Room 112." She pointed to somewhere behind her. "Just go through the intermediate ward here, and two hallways over starts the assisted living section. Do you want me to call her to let her know she has visitors? I know she'll be tickled. She doesn't get many visitors."

"No, we want to surprise her. We haven't seen her in so long. You just enjoy your time with Riff there. When we come back through, we'll go and visit with Mrs. Towers. You'll have Riff all to yourself for a couple of hours!"

"Great!" She grinned, and Riff panted her doggy smile in agreement.

Marcy Madsen Scrimger looked like a child all puddled up in a robe in the middle of a large easy chair; her tank of oxygen sat beside it. She stared at the Food Channel on TV. A lady was making some kind of cheese casserole mess. I rapped on the door several times before she glanced at the doorway. She didn't say anything, so I started, "Marcy Scrimger, are you Marcy Scrimger?"

Her head wobbled up and down on her thin neck. I felt ashamed griping about the inconvenience of having to wear a silken allergy mask for a few months each year when this poor, shriveled-up woman was spending the rest of her life tethered to an oxygen tank like Jacques Cousteau.

"May we come in?" I asked, and her head wobbled again.

"My name is Leslie Barrett, and this is my friend Belinda Honeycutt. We were talking with an old friend of yours yesterday. Do you remember Raymond Turner?"

"No," she said. At least I think she said it—her voice was so soft and dry I was going more by the movement of her lips than by sound.

She watched as we approached, stroking the oxygen tank like a lover, darting looks at the gauge. There weren't any other chairs in the room, so Belinda and I perched on the side of a twin bed facing Marcy.

I proceeded slowly, trying to keep my voice modulated. "Mrs. Scrimger, I don't know whether you've heard anything about the old barn out at your father's place."

Nostrils flared around the twin oxygen tubes pinching her nose, and her eyes darted around the room nervously.

"Were you aware that Denver's son sold the property?"

She shook her head and emitted a raspy "No."

I looked at Belinda, unsure of how to proceed. Belinda *tsk*ed. "Now, it isn't right that no one told you. After all, you grew up on that property. You should have been informed about the planned demolition of the barn."

Marcy's breath rattled fast and brittle through her open mouth. I leaned toward her and spoke softly. "The old Rambler was hauled out from under some rotten timbers, Marcy. There was a body in the trunk."

Tears ran from amazingly blue eyes down prematurely wrinkled cheeks. "Do you know who was in the trunk, Marcy? Do you know what happened to him?"

She blew out a breath that seemingly went on forever. "I… I…" She licked her lips and inhaled deeply. "I've waited forty-eight years to tell somebody what happened to Warren Keck out there in that old barn." She licked her lips. "It doesn't matter much now anyway. Denver's gone, and what happened to Warren was never my fault. Denver and I didn't know what to do. We knew it wasn't right just to leave Warren in the trunk like that. We were afraid nobody would believe that Denver never meant to hurt Warren."

"What happened to Warren, Marcy? The Tennessee Bureau of Investigation has Warren's body, and the Rambler has been gone over with a fine-tooth comb. They've started an investigation. If Belinda and I were able to track you down, so can the TBI. We know one of the bureau agents very well. If you tell us what happened to Warren, we can to explain everything to her. They're mainly concerned with identifying the body."

Marcy sighed heavily, causing a whistling noise through the tubes in her nose. "Well, the body in the trunk is Warren Keck." She sat back in the big chair, indicating she was settling in for a long story. "I don't get many visitors. Would you ladies like me to ask one of the attendants to bring you something to drink?"

I looked at Belinda, and she shook her head. "No, thank you," I answered for both of us. "If you want something though, go ahead and ring for it."

Patting the oxygen tank, she rasped a hoarse chuckle that sounded like it hurt. "I've got my liquid courage right here. Where do you want me to start?"

"At the beginning," I prompted.

"The beginning of what happened to Warren or the beginning of me?"

"Start with what happened to Warren."

"Warren Keck was twenty-three. The same age as my brother, Denver. Warren was handsome in a beat-up kind of way, if you know what I mean."

Belinda and I both nodded. "Bad-boy handsome?" I suggested.

She nodded. "He had that blue-black Elvis hair and the prettiest blue eyes I've ever seen. The combination was irresistible to my fifteen-year-old self. I was kind of a wild child back then, you know, pushing limits and stuff. My daddy and Denver tried to rein me in, but I enjoyed tugging on the reins too much. Warren was one of the bad boys around Clifton in those days. He got into a lot of fights with other guys. Denver punched him out once and told him to stay away from me, but that didn't stop us." She shrugged and sort of cackled. "All it did was push us closer together. Warren was always getting into trouble. He even told me that he and some other guy had broken into some houses to steal stuff to sell."

I found this an interesting tidbit. "Did he tell you anything specific, such as what homes, and what stuff?"

She shook her head, which caused the tubes to dance against the oxygen canister. "Nope, I didn't want to know any specifics even though Warren liked to brag about his exploits. Anyway, that old barn was old even forty-eight years ago. Daddy didn't use it for anything except storing junk. That old Rambler, for example. That car had been in the barn for ten years when Denver and I... Well, let me finish the story.

"Warren and I were fooling around in the hayloft one afternoon in the middle of summer, kid stuff, you know. I shouldn't have been surprised when Denver showed up, because Denver knew that I knew that the hayloft was one of Denver's favorite places to take his girls. He figured I would do the same. Denver was a good brother. He looked out for me. I didn't appreciate it much back then. I guess his protectiveness added an element of danger to messing around with Warren. I had no way of knowing just how much danger though. You know how people say 'Gosh, it all happened so fast?' Well, it did. We were rolling around in the hay up there in the loft when suddenly Denver was bellowing my name from below. While he was scrambling up the ladder to the loft, I was frantically pulling down the front of my blouse, and Warren was on his knees with his belt dangling open. Denver was mad as a wild boar—at both of us. He hauled Warren to his feet, his fists twisted in the fabric of Warren's shirt.

"I tried to reason with Denver. 'We were just fooling around, Denver. Honestly, nothing happened.' That kind of thing, but Denver was boiling mad. Warren didn't help matters much by smirking at Denver and grabbing at his wrists. Warren taunted him with something dumb like 'Nothing you can do about it, Madsen. Your sister has a mind of her own. She's gonna do, what she's gonna do.' Something really genius like that. Denver yowled, and the two of them went at it right up there in that hayloft. I tried to scoot out of the way. Denver was a good fighter. Pretty soon Warren was down on his stomach in the hay. Denver must have been totally out of his mind, because I couldn't believe it when he lifted Warren with one fist on the collar of his shirt and one on his loose belt and heaved Warren up in the air. You would have thought he was tossing him from a saloon or something. Warren flew through the air and landed on the hard-packed dirt floor of the barn. I screamed bloody murder, so did Warren, lot of good that did.

I didn't see Warren hit the floor. I heard it though. There was a loud, cracking *thud* and then silence. It wasn't like a thud and then scrambling around or anything. It was just that cracking *thud*. Then nothing.

"Denver stood at the edge of the loft as if he was in shock. He stood there for the longest time staring down at Warren. I crawled through the hay and looked down at Warren. He was just a lump lying down there; his neck was at a funny angle. It looked broken. Nothing had split open. There wasn't a pool of blood or anything like that. Just his neck looked all wrong."

Marcy shivered and swiped at the tears that had been dripping from her eyes.

"I remember I started crying something like 'Denver…what did you do? Oh my God, is Warren dead?' That seemed to snap him out of his frozen-in-place state, because he leaped to the top of the ladder, and the next thing I knew he was crouched beside Warren. He looked up at me with a look of horror that I had never seen before, and never saw again.

"I asked again if Warren was dead; all Denver did was nod. It's kind of funny now, but I remember asking Denver, 'What're we going to do? Daddy's going to kill us.' I mean, forget about our daddy; Denver could get lynched for killing Warren. We really scrambled around then. At first Denver thought about burying him out in the fields, but he worried about him getting dug up by one of the big farm machines. I was just a little-bitty thing, so there was no way I could help Denver dig a deep enough hole. That's when we got the idea of putting him in the trunk of that old Rambler. It wasn't easy, because the Rambler was backed up so close to the wall of the barn that I had to climb on top of the trunk, stick the key in the slot, and twist it back and forth until we heard the trunk latch give. I slid off the trunk, and Denver reached in to lift the lid. It wouldn't stay up without being held, so I slid across the top to the other side to hold it open while Denver dragged Warren over to the Rambler and hefted him up and in. It was bad. Warren hadn't been a real tall or fat guy. He was all ropy muscle. Still, Denver was sweating, and crying, by the time he let go, and the body thumped to the floor of the trunk. The tires were already all flat, so the car didn't rock or anything. It was just a loud, solid *glump* kind of sound. Denver was crying really hard by this time, and he motioned for me to let go of the trunk; but I sobbed, "No, Denver, don't leave him like that. We have to at least cover him with something.

"I don't think Denver was able to think by then. He took hold of the trunk lid and held it open and made shooing motions. I squeezed around the car, remembering one of Mamaw's old quilts had been up in the hayloft for forever. I climbed up the ladder, dragged the quilt from the loft, and tossed it past Denver and into the trunk. Denver reached down to straighten the quilt so that the only things showing were Warren's boots. Then he let go of the lid, and it slammed shut with a loud bang. We covered the car again with the heavy tarp Daddy had thrown over it years earlier. We tossed some dirt on top of the tarp so it wouldn't look like anybody had been messing with it.

"We sat on the floor of that old barn, crying and holding on to one another like two terrified children."

Marcy cleared her throat and started coughing. Belinda got up and poured a glass of water from a pitcher on the nightstand. Accepting the glass, she took a sip and strangled out a thank you.

"This is going to sound strange, but that afternoon in the barn, Denver and I had never been so close before or since. We promised each other that we would never tell anyone what happened to Warren, and we didn't until now. It doesn't matter anymore 'cause Denver's dead. Can't nobody try to arrest him or anything."

Frowning, I asked, "So no one ever came looking for Warren?"

With one shake of her head, Marcy said, "Not really, there were some rumblings about, you know, 'Wonder where Warren went,' but nobody much cared. Warren wasn't from around here. He just showed up one day, so it wasn't that weird for him just to go away again. Denver was worried about one guy who seemed more interested than anyone else, but even he finally quit coming around asking people what happened to Warren."

This next question had to be phrased with social work delicacy. "And… um… the smell never became a problem?"

She shook her head vigorously, causing the tubes to dance once again. "Like I told you, Daddy wasn't using that old barn for anything except to shove junk into it. There wasn't any reason for anyone to actually go very far into the barn. All the men working for Daddy had to do was open the doors long enough to chuck something inside then close them up again. I imagine there was a lot of junk coming out of that barn before they ever got back to where that old Rambler sat."

Belinda nodded. "That's true. I recall seeing a couple of washers or dryers, a bunch of wood–like you said, junk."

"Yeah, we never went there again. I can promise you that. Funny, but after a while we kind of forgot about Warren being in that old Rambler. I didn't mess around so much with boys after that. Got married to Lou a couple of years later. Lou was a good man. We raised two boys together; too bad they don't come to visit their old mother very often, but they are good boys. Lou died when he got pinned beneath a tractor. I never could figure out what he was trying to fix under there, but it sure fixed Lou. After Lou died Daddy took care of the boys and me. Then after Daddy died Denver was always there for us. Denver married Lacy Thompson, and they had a boy and a girl. The boy, Fred, inherited the property when Denver died last year. Denver had three heart attacks before the last one took him home. I didn't know Fred had sold off the last ten acres of Daddy's property to the Glen people. Can't blame him much though; wasn't doing the family any good."

We were quiet for a long time until I asked, "Marcy, what can you tell us about the key?"

She removed the cannulas from her nostrils, wiped them off with a towel she held in her lap, put them back in, and asked, "What key?"

"I found a small key on top of the quilt. It has some markings on it that look like it may have been for something out at Tennessee Central Railway."

"That old railroad? There was a lot of excitement about it for a while, but it never came to anything. The old depot is some kind of gift shop or something now."

"Did Warren or your brother work for the railroad or maybe hang around out there around the time of Warren's accident?"

"No, not that I know of. Denver was working in one of Daddy's banks by that time. Warren didn't work at anything except breaking into people's houses and stealing stuff."

"So you don't know anything about the key or what it unlocks?"

"Nope."

Belinda had listened while I asked all the questions, until now. "I'm curious  how you got the trunk of the car open if you didn't have the key."

I looked at my friend in admiration. "Good question."

"The keys were in the glove box. Denver told me later that he had dropped the keys down an abandoned well on the property."

I probed, "When you and your brother first opened the trunk of the Rambler, did you notice anything in the trunk?"

With a shake of her head, she said, "No, we were pretty much not seeing anything by that time. Later on we got to wondering whether we should have checked Warren's pockets more thoroughly for identification or cash, but by then Denver had already gotten rid of the keys to the car." She shuddered. "I'm not sure either of us would have had enough gumption to reopen that trunk anyway."

"What do you mean when you say you should have checked his pockets more thoroughly? Did you check his pockets?"

"No. When Warren fell, some coins and stuff fell out of his pockets and onto the barn floor. Denver picked up everything and tossed it in the trunk before slamming the lid shut. I suppose there may have been a key of some kind, but I never saw it."

Belinda and I exchanged knowing glances. I asked, "Did you happen to notice what stuff had spilled from Warren's pockets?"

"Not really, just some coins, oh, and the keys to his car. He had one of those Playboy Bunny key chains. I remember Denver picking it up. He took the car keys so he could dispose of Warren's car, and, like I said, the rest he just tossed into the trunk."

"You said earlier Denver worked at your father's bank. Did he collect coins by any chance? I mean, like old or special coins?"

She shook her head. "No, Denver didn't give a flip about numismatics."

"Come again?"

"Numismatics: the study and collecting of old coins. Denver didn't care about any money he couldn't spend. Why?"

"We found a 1964 Kennedy half-dollar wedged in the well where a spare tire would normally have been kept. It was in a little plastic display sleeve."

"Right. To preserve the coin." She gave a thoughtful nod and sucked in a hit of oxygen. "I don't know how that coin came to be in the trunk."

I felt an aha moment coming on. "So, Marcy, was your father one of those numis-whatsits?"

"Oh no. Daddy didn't care about old coins. He got catalogs for collectors though. Pretty boring stuff actually. I spent my entire life listening to Daddy and Denver talk about money stuff. I don't know anything about numismatics either. I just remember the term."

My aha moment had been a dead end.

Belinda wondered, "What did Denver do with Warren's car?"

Marcy shrugged. "It wasn't much of a car. I don't recall where Denver told me he left it. I know that he removed the license plate and threw it and the car keys down the well I told you about."

I hopped off the bed, and Belinda rocked to a standing position. I offered my hand to Marcy. "Thank you, Marcy Madsen Scrimger. This will be one cold case the TBI can put to bed."

Belinda shook her hand also. "Thank you, Mrs. Scrimger."

Squinting into my eyes, Marcy asked, "Am I going to be in trouble?"

"We can't promise anything, but I doubt it. Obviously, you shouldn't have helped stuff Warren in that trunk, but I understand why you did it."

"He was my brother. It was an accident."

"I know."

As we were leaving, we turned back at Marcy's call. "Ladies, would you come and visit me again?  I'd really appreciate it."

Belinda and I glanced at one another, then nodded . "Sure, Marcy, we'll come by from time to time," I said.

"And Raymond, tell Ray Turner to come and see me."

I grinned. "So you do remember Raymond Turner."

Marcy pursed her lips. "Yeah, Denver beat up Ray once or twice."

Threading our way back toward the reception desk, Belinda announced to the hallway, "Boy, that was one sad story."

I looked into the distance. "Yup, sad. The key must have been one of the things that spilled from Warren's pockets after his high dive. At least that explains what it was doing lying on top of the quilt. We still don't know where he got it or what it goes to though." I threw my hands at the ceiling. "And that stupid coin doesn't seem to have anything to do with anything!"

"The mystery is never over for you, is it, Les? At least now you know the man in the trunk isn't Elvis."

I sighed. "Like Yogi Berra said, 'It ain't over till it's over.' We need to solve the mystery of the key, so it ain't over."

We rounded the corner by the reception desk and smiled at the little crowd of fans adoring Riff. She threw me a look that seemed to say, "Enough already. Get me outta here."

We passed Mrs. Turley huddled with her daughter in the lobby. Over the sound of Belinda's clomping boot, I heard Liz say, "Mom, tell me that funny story again about when Daddy played Santa Claus at the neighborhood party."

I nodded at Liz, and she smiled in return. Belinda said out of the corner of her mouth, "Score one for Leslie."

"And Mrs. Turley."

"And her daughter."

# Chapter Sixteen

Belinda rapped on Mrs. Towers' door, and we entered to discover her scowling into a bowl of some kind of soup. "Girls, thank God you've come. I can't get anyone to call for that discharge order. I asked the nurse *again,* and she said she would ask the social worker *again.* What the #&&%! That little social worker can't keep me here. She isn't my boss, nor is she my doctor. Leslie, what in the world did you do to your bangs?"

"Don't worry about them."

"They're all crooked."

I huffed irritably, "Why don't you call your doctor yourself?"

I was rewarded with a wide grin that caused her eyes to sparkle. "I did!"

"And?" asked Belinda.

"I couldn't get past his nurse, but she listened to me and said she would pass along the message that I wanted him to call in a discharge order. Seriously, girls, where have you been all day? Leslie, you need to get Regina to fix your hair."

I ignored her. "We paid a visit to the assisted living wing of this fine establishment."

Hands flying to her face, Mrs. Towers wailed, "Oh noooooo! Who put you up to that? Valerie or that horrid little social worker? *Karen* has been badgering me to tour that wing. I won't do it. I won't. There may come a time when I need that much help, but that time is not now."

She folded her arms in defiance.

"Don't worry, we weren't checking out potential new digs for you or anything. We just paid a visit to a resident over there."

"Who?"

"We can talk about that later. Do you really feel as though you can manage at home?" I asked warily. Mrs. Towers would either reassure me or bite my head off. Fortunately, I was reassured.

"Yes, I do. I explained to the doctor's nurse about home health PT for strengthening—as you girls said—and also told her I have two wonderful neighbors who will look in on me faithfully. I told her about the protein drinks, and that I promised to carry my help-gizmo with me everywhere."

"Oh, that reminds me." I dug around in my purse and came up with the plastic carrying case with its Velcro strap. "I bought you a present. I figured you could strap it to your walker and keep your help-gizmo in it. You're never very far from your walker."

Belinda laughed. "Yeah, you can keep your help-gizmo in it or your .38."

"Belinda," she said with a straight face, "I carry a .22."

When rewarded by our panicked faces, Mrs. Towers pointed her index finger and snapped her thumb. "*Bang.* Gotcha! So, are you girls going to get me out of here or not?"

I reassured Mrs. Towers, "Your doctor won't have a problem with a discharge order. It's just a matter of him getting the time to call it in. Nursing homes and home health agencies have a kind of love/hate relationship. Everyone wants those Medicare bucks. Your doctor won't be swayed by that though. All he'll care about is that you have what you need at home."

Pushing the lap tray off to the side of the bed, she swung her legs to the ground and snapped her walker in front of her like she was twirling a lasso. "Let's go."

Belinda rocked back on her boot. "You don't have a discharge order yet."

"I don't care. You heard Leslie. It's just a matter of time. I'll leave them a note."

Belinda threw me a stricken face, but I was grinning through my raggedy bangs. "I've always wanted to break somebody out of one of these places. I'm in." I did a fist pump for emphasis.

Mrs. Towers aimed a challenging face at my friend. "Belinda, you in? If not, go get Riff and meet us at the car."

With a big, loud flap of both arms, Belinda replied, "Well, to heck with it. Why not? The two of you are going to do it anyway, but how are we going to get you out of here without being stopped?"

"Mrs. Towers needs a disguise. If we come up with a good one, she can walk right out the front door." I tapped fingers to my lips. "We'll need a distraction." I shook off that part of the plan to focus on the disguise. Mrs. Towers was wearing a hot-pink sweatsuit and her sensible white walking shoes. I looked down at my feet. I was wearing my green Keds with matching green laces. I like to match my laces to my shoes; it's a recent fashion quirk of mine. I love Keds. I keep a variety of colors of them lined up in my closet. Between my blue Keds and my black Indigo pumps rests Tom's cremains in a tasteful box with his name and dates of birth and death engraved on a small metallic plate. I probably could have skipped the engraving expense. It's not like I have boxes of other dead people hanging out in my closet.

"I've got an idea. We can swap my green shoelaces for your white ones."

"With hot pink?" Mrs. Towers shook her head. "I don't think so, Leslie."

"What about that bright-yellow outfit you had on yesterday? Where is it?"

She waved her arm. "It's in that laundry bag next to the chair."

"Belinda, dig out her yellow outfit. We can make that work with the green laces." Belinda grumbled as she headed toward the chair.

Once we had Mrs. Towers' outfitted, we stood back to look at her. Belinda *tsk*ed. "She's still very obviously Mrs. Towers."

I had an epiphany. "I know." I dug enthusiastically in my purse and came up twirling my allergy mask around my index finger. "Freshly washed and everything," I boasted.

"Oh, that's a good idea. People will avoid me like the plague."

"Leslie, we have to hide her hair somehow. That white head of hers almost glows."

"Don't let Leslie anywhere near me with a pair of scissors. I have a rain bonnet in my purse."

"No good," I said. "It isn't raining."

"I have a scarf too. With another wave of her hand, she ordered, "Hand me my purse from that drawer over there."

She pulled out a small white scarf. "Will this help?"

"I probably shouldn't be encouraging this deception," Belinda mused.

"What, *what*?" Mrs. Towers and I both encouraged.

"Well, I have some brown eye shadow in my purse." She cast a critical eye at Mrs. Towers. "What if she wears your mask, and we tie the scarf around her head and pull some of her hair around her face. If we dust her hair with the brown eye shadow, she won't look like a little old lady. She'll look like the devil, but less like someone about to bust out of an old folks home."

We grinned at each other impishly, admiring our handiwork in the mirror over the bathroom vanity. "They won't be expecting to see you in that yellow outfit again. That hot-pink number you had on is probably burned into their retinas. If we can come up with a distraction, this just might work. What did you write in your note?" I asked.

Mrs. Towers read aloud the note she'd placed on her pillow.

"Dear Nurse, I called my doctor. He will call you with discharge orders. I am going home now. Thanks for everything. Sincerely yours, Elizabeth Towers"

"That sounds pretty good. It implies you knew you had the doctor's permission to leave. Kind of stick it a little under your pillow though; that way they won't find it right away."

Belinda frowned at me in the mirror. "What about a distraction?"

The purse lady appeared in the bathroom door, peering through the crowd in the mirror. "Have any of you ladies seen Mitch Turley?"

I whirled around. "Hi, Mrs. Turley, are you looking for Mitch again?"

"Leslie…" Belinda's warning voice sounded.

"Mrs. Turley, how about I help you look for your husband." I backed her off a few steps from the bathroom door where she waited patiently, purse in the crook of one arm.

"Leslie…"

I huddled with my coconspirators, whispering, "Mrs. Towers, you know that exit door at the end of the hall, the one with the warning alarm?"

"Sure, Missy walks me down the hall, and we loop back when we reach that door. But it has a huge sign that says 'ALARM WILL SOUND IF DOOR IS OPENED.' A person would have to be crazy to open that door."

"Not crazy, confused. Alarming the exits is a safety precaution in case purse ladies wander off. Once the alarm goes off, the staff will swarm the grounds searching for the wanderer."

Belinda frowned. "I don't think I like where you're going with this, Les."

"Look, all we need is a distraction. Once Mrs. Turley opens that door the alarm will sound, everybody goes running, and we make our escape through the front entrance."

I pointed at Mrs. Towers. "You follow us like you're supposed to be there. Don't throw your walker in front of you, dragging yourself behind it like an old lady. Walk as quickly and confidently as possible, like you're a visitor. Follow us to my car. Hopefully, we can get away in all the confusion."

"I can't manage without my walker, Leslie."

"I didn't say you can't use the walker. All I'm saying is try not to look feeble."

"I'm not feeble."

"Okay," Belinda mumbled, looking toward the bedroom. "Leslie, the purse lady is gone!"

I hurried into the bedroom and found Mrs. Turley sitting in a chair by the door, patiently waiting. "Are you ready, dear?" she asked with a beatific smile.

I walked Mrs. Turley toward the exit door at the end of the hallway. "Mrs. Turley, I think Mitch may have gone through this door. It makes a loud noise when the door is opened but just push on through. It won't hurt anything. It's just noise."

"Oh, thank you, dear. I've been looking everywhere for that man." Mrs. Turley walked toward the door at a determined clip. Without pausing, she gave a loud grunt, smacked the bar on the door, and vanished with a loud "*WHOOP WHOOP WHOOP!*"

Sure enough, the staff all went running. I pinwheeled my arm at my friends to hurry. Belinda and I scurried to the front entrance while Mrs. Towers followed behind. Holding my hands out for Riff, the receptionist handed her over while craning her neck to see through the glass doors.

"Whatever is going on?" I widened my actress eyes in wonder.

"One of the patients seems to have wandered off," she replied distractedly.

"Oh dear," I *tsk*ed to Belinda sympathetically. "Come on, let's get out of the way and let these people do their jobs."

Mrs. Towers coughed lightly through the silk mask. I tossed her a look and noticed a brown dusting on my allergy mask, no doubt the result of the quick eye shadow hair dye job. Her disguise reminded me of one that Carol Burnett wore on her show years ago. A giggle threatened, but I choked it down.

Belinda and I walked through the front doors. Nurses and attendants swarmed the parking lot. I snagged the arm of a nurse. "Excuse me, nurse. I saw an old lady with shiny white hair in a hot-pink outfit dragging herself behind a walker. She was headed that way." I pointed to a far corner of the building. "I thought I should mention it."

"Oh, thank you," she gushed, running to some of the other staff. They turned like a school of those silver fish in *Finding Nemo* and galloped in the new direction.

We passed Mrs. Turley in the parking lot. She whisked into the building via the front doors in full mission mode.

"Guess she didn't find Mitch," Belinda said in a low voice.

Sucking in my lips, I managed to avoid the manic laugh that threatened; a manic snort escaped nonetheless. Handing Riff off to Belinda, we approached the Soul. I unlocked the doors with the key fob, opened the rear-passenger door, tossed Mrs. Towers' walker into the backseat, and she crawled in behind it. We were like the pit crew at a Nascar race.

"Lie down on the seat, Mrs. Towers. We don't want anyone to see you or catch us on surveillance cameras with your head bobbing around in the backseat," I ordered brusquely.

She flattened herself on the seat, whipping off the silk mask, and shook her head. Powdery-brown dust motes filled the air.

"Don't get brown eye shadow all over the upholstery." I groaned.

Mrs. Towers whooped with laughter and shook a fist. "Those lousy screws couldn't keep me penned up!"

We all started laughing with relief while Riff barked along. We pulled it off! After traveling two blocks with no sirens on our tail, Belinda leaned her head back and shouted, "*YA-HOO!*" Belinda is not normally the yahoo type, so this really brought on the pee-in-your-drawers laughter. That's when I saw the green truck.

I slapped Belinda's arm to get her attention. "Belinda. Belinda..."

Finally, she calmed down enough to sputter, "What?"

"I saw that green truck again, back there at the last intersection. It pulled out behind us–see it?"

Wiping the streaming tears from her eyes, she squinted in the passenger-side mirror. "Okay, I see a green truck, so what? Do you know how many beat-up old green trucks there are around here? Almost as many as there are white Kia ice-cream trucks."

Mrs. Towers' head appeared in my rearview mirror. "Mrs. Towers, keep down!" I barked. Her head disappeared.

"What truck?" she hollered.

Belinda groaned. "Oh, Leslie has it in her head that we're being followed by a green truck."

"Why would anyone be following you? Leslie, do you think it has anything to do with that skeleton you found in that old car? I remember the Nash Rambler— what a great little car. She started singing "Little Nash Rambler."

When she trailed off into humming because she couldn't remember the words, Belinda answered for me, "No, it doesn't have anything to do with the man in the trunk, Mrs. Towers. Leslie is having one of her pesky delusions again."

I harrumphed, but I didn't have any concrete evidence to the contrary.

Belinda's cell phone started to ring, and she fished around in her purse for it. Checking the display she said, "It's Valerie."

"Don't answer it. Don't answer it!" Mrs. Towers' head popped back up. "They found my note and put out one of those APDs on me."

"You mean an APB—all points bulletin—and keep your head down." When the ringing stopped, the phone started making that dinging noise that signals a voice message. Then my cell phone started ringing.

"Don't answer it!" Mrs. Towers head reappeared in the mirror.

"I'm not going to answer it. Sheesh, keep your shorts on. I expect they'll get the doctor's order by the end of the day. We'll simply tell everyone that we were under the impression you had permission to leave, which is *close* to the truth."

We were closing in on the Glen, but I didn't even slow down for the turnoff. "Where are you going?" Belinda asked.

"I want to get another look at that hayloft."

"Leslie, no. That old barn is going to fall down around your ears."

Mrs. Towers' head appeared and then disappeared. "The barn with the skeleton? What's going on?"

We told Mrs. Towers about our visit with Marcy Scrimger and how we now knew the identity of the man in the trunk, and how he had gotten there.

"Wow, how cool is that? Leslie, you need to call that TBI lady." Mrs. Towers headless voice floated over the headrests, "Boy, she's going to be fit to be tied when she finds out you girls scooped her again!"

"Leslie, turn around. Let's go home and call Agent Donnelly or Chief Braddock, " Belinda pleaded.

Mrs. Towers snorted derisively. "Sheriff Braddock isn't going to do anything. He's as touchy as that TBI lady when it comes to you and Leslie. I vote we check out the hayloft."

Belinda whipped her head around to address Mrs. Towers. "Not you too! That old barn is falling down. There isn't anything to be learned by going out there. We already know what happened."

"Why, what happened?" Mrs. Towers asked.

I kept driving while I filled in the details about Warren Keck, and how he came to be stuffed into the trunk of the old Rambler. I finished, "All I want to do is confirm that a fall from that hayloft could have resulted in Warren's death."

"Obviously, it could because it did," Belinda said bluntly.

"That barn has been standing there for a hundred years. It isn't going to go into some kind of Stephen King–induced epileptic fit just because I walk into it."

We had reached the northern perimeter of the Glen. I turned off onto the series of dirt roads that lead to the clearing, and the barn. I parked about twenty feet from the barn and switched off the ignition. "You guys stay here. This will only take a minute."

Belinda shook her head defiantly. "Oh no you don't. Don't you dare go all Lone Ranger on me. I'm going with you."

"You're wearing that balloon boot; just wait here for me."

"No."

I huffed, "Fine." Mrs. Towers' head appeared, and I said, "No, Mrs. Towers, you and Riff wait for us. We'll only be a few minutes."

She returned to her reclining position with Riff sprawled at her side. When we opened our doors, Riff started scrabbling to follow. Mrs. Towers quieted her. "Sorry, Riff; we escaped convicts have to lay low."

Belinda and I crossed the grass and moved from the sunlight into the shadow of the barn. "Boy, it's dark in here"—I coughed—"and dry."

I walked deeper into the structure, which had been emptied enough that I could stand near the hayloft ladder. Remarkably, there were still old bales of hay strewn about like big dust bunnies. We stood looking up at the hayloft. "Belinda, you're almost six feet tall; go stand beneath the hayloft so I can guesstimate how high it is."

Snapping her head to meet my eyes, she huffed, "I will not. I'm not going to stand under that rickety old loft like your personal yardstick. I can eyeball it from here. It has to be at least twelve feet up. Just how far are you willing to go to reenact said event? Why don't you climb up that rotten ladder and fling yourself from the hayloft? If you die of a broken neck, we'll have our proof."

"Is that how Warren Keck died?" A young man's voice offered the question, and we staggered around in surprise, reaching for each other. The silhouette of a lean man pointing a rifle materialized in the doorway, backlit by the sunny day. Ridiculously he ordered, "Put your hands up."

# Chapter Seventeen

Belinda and I fumbled apart and reached for the sky. I yelped, "Don't shoot!"

It felt like we were in a bad episode of *The Rifleman*. Although the young man was clearly trying to sound tough, a tremor in his voice belied his nervousness. As the young man crossed from sunlight to shadow, he hitched a bag higher on a shoulder. He was just a boy, young, whip-thin, with sandy hair going every which way beneath a John Deere cap. He wore blue jeans and a dirt-smudged, used-to-be-white t-shirt, and scuffed his boots across the dirt, kicking up dust as he walked toward us.

I noticed a low, slinking shape backlit at the door. As it drew closer, I realized it was an old hound. The poor thing shuffled across the floor of the barn to flop down in a heap behind the boy.

"I assume you're a Tennessee boy," I called to him. "You have the shotgun and the dog. I'm guessing that was your green truck following us."

Belinda's breath was hitching in her throat, and I glanced at her with concern "You're scaring my friend, young man, and I don't appreciate it."

He took a step closer and asked gruffly, "What happened to Warren Keck?"

Belinda's voice came out in a strangled mewl. "It's a long story."

I flicked my eyes to hers. "No, it isn't."

"Leslie?"

"Look, young man, this property used to belong to Cecil Madsen. Back in 1968, Cecil's boy, Denver, caught his little sister and Warren Keck canoodling in the hayloft. Denver went crazy and tossed Warren headfirst from the hayloft. Once the kids knew Warren was dead, they panicked and stuffed him into the trunk of an old car that had been abandoned in this barn. The barn is being torn down, the car was dragged from the barn, and I convinced the wrecker service to jimmy the trunk lock with a screwdriver. Ta-da, we discovered the dusty remains of Warren Keck. Now, what do *you* know about Warren Keck, and what's your name?"

The boy stood silently, his fingers flexing nervously on the gun.

"Okay," I called to him, "then what's the name of your dog?"

The boy muttered something that I couldn't make out.

"Excuse me?"

"Rover," he growled.

"Hello, Rover," I addressed the dog, still holding my arms in the air.

"He can't hear you. Rover's old. His hearing is about gone," the boy said.

"*HELLO, ROVER!*" I screamed.

My scream made the boy jump. "Crap, lady, what's wrong with you?"

"What's *wrong* with me? What's wrong with *me*? Well, some darn fool kid is pointing a shotgun at me. Now, what's your name?" I barked.

"Shut up," he called out with bluster. "You don't need to know my name."

Belinda's voice went all wheedling and girly-quivery. "Look, son, we didn't mean to trespass in your barn. We'll leave. No harm done."

The boy's eyes never left mine.

"Belinda, this boy has been following us all day. His interest in us doesn't have anything to do with trespassing." I narrowed my eyes. "It has to do with Warren Keck."

"You don't know he was following us, Leslie. It could have been your imagination. My arms are tired. Besides, I never heard of Warren Keck."

"My name is Leslie Barrett and this lady telling you a fib is my friend Belinda."

"I know who you are," he said through gritted teeth, drilling my eyes with his.

I couldn't help tossing a satisfied glance at Belinda. "Told you we were being followed." Then, addressing the boy, I said, "It isn't fair that you know our names but we don't know yours. Our arms are getting tired, son; we're old ladies. I don't see any reason to withhold your name, assuming you plan to shoot us, tired arms and all, with that shotgun." I aimed my chin at the rifle. "I'm going to need your name in order to give God an accurate accounting of what transpired here. He's going to want to know why I prematurely appeared at the pearly gates. I want to make sure I have your name right."

Belinda shuffled closer and whispered a warning. "Leslie, what are you doing?"

In my regular voice I said, "I'm trying to find out what's bothering this young man, Belinda, before he kills us." I told the boy, "I'm putting my arms down. Go ahead and shoot if you want." I lowered my arms to my sides with bravado.

That stymied him. "What...?"

Belinda lowered her arms with a slow, relieved sigh.

"I like the name of your dog, Rover," I continued to blather, "That's an excellent name. Did you know that rover is another word for *rambler*. If you look up *rambler* in a thesaurus, *rover* will be listed as a synonym, you know, like *vagabond*, *wanderer*, and so on. Don't you find that a funny coincidence? I mean, we find Warren Keck in the trunk of a Rambler, and your dog's name is Rover."

The boy asked, "What's a thesaurus?"

"It's a book, kind of like a dictionary. Sounds like the name of a dinosaur, doesn't it?" I knew I was jabbering, but I couldn't seem to stop. "Are you threatening us with that gun because we found Warren Keck in the trunk of the Rambler? What does Warren Keck have to do with you, son? You weren't even on this earth when Warren Keck went into that trunk."

Riff came around the corner and into the barn like a yapping, white dust storm. Rover didn't even twitch, but the boy swung the shotgun around and *BLOOEY!*

I screamed at Belinda, "*Get down!*" I was about to collapse onto the dirt floor in a heap, as Belinda dived to her right. Riff was coming fast, and when the boy aimed at my dog, I flung myself at him in a rolling fury and smacked the boy in his knees. He fell backward over me and *BLOOEY!* Another blast from the gun went into the rafters of the barn. I grappled the rifle from his hands and started walking on my knees across the hard-packed dirt toward the bales of hay—"*Ow, ow, ow*"— while jerking the rifle back and forth. Trying to raise myself to my feet with the assist of a hay bale, I jerked my head around at the sound of Mrs. Towers' threatening tone. "I would stay down if I were you, boy."

Mrs. Towers loomed above the boy, straddling him with her walker. She had removed the scarf, and her face was smeared with brown eye shadow. Clad in that bright-yellow sweatsuit and white shoes with green shoelaces, she looked like one of those M&M people on the commercials.

Riff had abandoned her attack and was whimpering from behind some hay bales. All I could see of Belinda was the toe of her balloon boot poking above the bale. Once I grunted myself to a standing position, I limped toward Mrs. Towers and handed the shotgun off to her. "You cover him, Mrs. Towers. I've got to check on Belinda." I quickly limped around the hay bales. "Belinda, Belinda!" My best friend in the whole world was lying on the dirt floor, out, stone cold. I started patting her cheeks and crooning. I wanted to kneel at her side, but I didn't think I could get back up. I let out a small, involuntary sob of relief when she started moaning.

I limp-stomped around the hay bale toward the boy, who sat on the barn floor. Mrs. Towers planted herself several feet away, the shotgun resting on her walker.

I screamed, "*WHAT IN SAM HILL IS WRONG WITH YOU, BOY? YOU COULD HAVE KILLED US! BELINDA KNOCKED HERSELF SILLY FALLING ON THIS HARD-PACKED DIRT! ARE YOU OUT OF YOUR FREAKING MIND? WE'RE OLD LADIES, FOR HEAVEN'S SAKE!*"

Gone was any pretense at bluster or toughness as he pleaded, "Look, I'm sorry. I was just trying to scare you into telling me where Warren hid the money. Those weren't even real bullets. They're blanks, cheap blanks at that. How am I going to kill anybody with blanks? They make noise, and that's all!" Hooking a small backpack with one foot, he hitched it to his side.

"Watch it!" Mrs. Towers ordered.

"I'm showing you they were blanks." Upending the backpack, he dumped the contents in the dirt. Red tubes tumbled from a box.

Mrs. Towers leaned in and hollered over her shoulder, "The box says they're tracer shells. He's telling the truth."

"How do you know?" I asked skeptically.

"Arnie played a Yankee in a couple of Civil War reenactments in Franklin, Tennessee. The North still won. Anyway, I remember Arnie showing off the ammunition to me. He was like a kid." Arnie was Mrs. Tower's late husband.

Riff had abandoned Belinda and was sniffing around the old, lumpy dog, Rover. Rover didn't acknowledge her. Mrs. Towers, holding the rifle with one hand while balancing it across the top bar of her walker, stumped toward the boy. Leaning down, she removed her other hand from the walker long enough to swat the boy on the side of his head. *"You dang fool kid! Tracers are still dangerous!"*

Belinda's moaning grew louder, and I returned to her side to help her to her feet. Once vertical, she started to sway, and we both almost went down. I nudged her around the bales and propped her against them.

Hand to her head, she mumbled, "Wha' happened?"

"Looks like you hit your head. You may have a concussion. Let me see your eyes."

Belinda lowered her eyes to mine; too bad I had no idea what I was looking for. It's just something people say as if they know what eyes look like when there's a concussion lurking behind them. I don't know what concussed eyes look like. "How do you feel?"

"Woozy, sick, and my head hurts. Leslie, what happened?"

I pointed to the boy who still sat with his back against the mangled bale. "That boy is the one who's been following us. He was shooting at us!"

The boy cried, "Blanks—I showed you—they were blanks."

I watched as the dog, Rover, creaked to his feet, ambled over to the boy, and dropped to his side with a weary breath.

*The dog loves him, so the kid can't be all bad.*

Riff followed Rover to the boy and proceeded to sniff both of them thoroughly.

Mrs. Towers made a couple of stumping steps in our direction. "Leslie, I called the sheriff when I saw the boy follow you in here with that gun. I told the 911 lady we were out at the barn where you found the dead body. I couldn't remember the name of the owner."

I sniffed the air and realized the boy had lit a cigarette. He was sucking on it like Marcy had on the oxygen—how ironic. "Put out that cigarette!" I barked. "This old barn is a tinderbox. What's the matter with you? Don't you know cigarettes will kill you?"

The boy stabbed the cigarette in the dirt, then tossed it behind him. "Sorry," he mumbled grouchily. "What are you going to tell the police about me?"

I asked Mrs. Towers to join Belinda. She moved across the barn floor, continuing to glare at the young man, and settled beside Belinda, the shotgun at her side like a pioneer woman. Both women gripped a handle of Mrs. Towers' walker. They looked like crap. Belinda was glassy-eyed and had straw stuck in her hair. Mrs. Towers' face and white hair were smeared with brown eye shadow. They were leaning on the hay bales, Mrs. Towers' walker, and each other.

I answered the boy. "We don't know about you yet. Who are you, how old are you, and what was all this about? You'd better tell me quickly. The posse will be here shortly."

He looked so dejected slumped there with one old dog flopped on his lap and Riff lying across one ankle like she had him trapped.

"Can I stand up?"

I nodded at the dogs. "That depends on those two."

The boy gently lifted Rover's head from his lap, scooted his butt over, and settled the dog's head on the dirt floor. Riff growled low in her throat.

"Riff," I called, "come here, Tiger."

Riff didn't seem too sure that it was a good idea to let go of her prisoner, so I added: "He's all right, he isn't going to hurt anybody." That seemed to satisfy her, and she trotted to my side. I leaned over and one-handed her into my arms. I kissed the top of her head, and she got one good lick on my cheek, which I hate. "Blech, okay, okay."

The boy stood and walked toward me, stopping about five feet away. "My name is Marty Christmas."

I lifted both eyebrows, mainly because my eyebrows don't work independently of one another. "Marty Christmas? Really? What a cool name."

Marty looked at his feet, then back up at me with a small, sad smile.

"You need to hurry up, Marty. Tell me what's going on."

"Yeah, okay. Where do you want me to start?"

"Tell us what prompted you to follow us today."

He flexed his wrists nervously. "I live alone with my mom; my dad took off when I was born. They were just teenagers, never married, and my mom said she wasn't surprised when he split. That's why she didn't give me his last name. It's been just the two of us since my Grandpa Daniels died. Grandpa was my dad's father. He wasn't much, Grandpa, I mean, but other than my mom, he was the only family I had. Anyway, we live in his crummy old trailer, and my mom works a lot of hours as a waitress. I'm sixteen, so I've got my driver's license and Grandpa Daniels' old truck."

Marty's story was interrupted when a wave of heat rolled over the hay bale and smoke billowed. He grabbed his dog and dived away from the smoldering hay bale. I froze for about one-half second just staring at the smoke. Then the flames erupted and began to lick up the rotten wood of one of the horse stalls. As is my normal atavistic response to terror, I sucked in a huge lungful of nasty-tasting smoke. It went down my throat and up my nose like an alien entity.

"*Marty,*" I yelled, half strangling on the sand-colored smoke, "*that cigarette, we have to get out of here! This place will be an ashtray in about forty seconds!*" I pulled the top of my shirt up to my face as a filter. What a time to be without my mask.

Belinda shrieked a hoarse, panicked "*LESLIE-E-E-E!*" She and Mrs. Towers were staggering against one another, the walker threatening to trip them both.

Marty scrambled to his feet and shouted to Rover, "*ROVER…RUN, BOY!*"

Rover did the best he could…last I saw he was headed in the right direction.

I ran to Belinda and Mrs. Towers. The hay bales where Marty had been resting were ablaze, and smoke fogged the barn.

Marty ran to us and yelled around the smoke, "*YOU GET THE OLD LADY! I'LL GET THE TALL ONE!*"

I met his eyes uncertainly but moved when he barked roughly, "*GO AHEAD! MOVE!*"

I tugged Mrs. Towers away from the hay bale, slapped her hands on the handles of her walker, and coughed. "We have to get out of here, Mrs. Towers."

Mrs. Towers didn't need much encouragement, but she was wobbling and wilting fast. With Riff in one arm, I wrapped my other around Mrs. Towers' waist and nudged her through the smoke toward the open barn doors. Without my shirt filter, the smoke curled into a solid mass inside my chest like a lazy cat. Marty was still yelling at Rover and grappling with Belinda.

Once we were outside, I led Mrs. Towers away from the burning barn, tears streaming from our eyes. When we were several feet away, I heard the unmistakable creaking and crashing from the depths of the barn. It was coming down—*now*—and in flames.

I shoved Riff into Mrs. Towers' arms, croaking, "Take Riff and keep going. I've got to get Belinda!"

My brave, elderly friend didn't hesitate. She tucked Riff under her arm and one-handed the walker away from the inferno. I had already turned and was halfway back to the barn entrance when Marty appeared, supporting Belinda's tall, stumbling form. It was a surreal sight: the smoke erupting from the barn doors in giant waves.

I ran toward Marty and Belinda sobbing in relief, "Thank God!" I tucked myself beneath Belinda's other arm, and Marty and I led her away from the smoke, her balloon boot dragging in the dust. The smoke and debris were like a tornado—straight up in the air.

In the distance I saw a dust storm approaching with sirens blaring. I left Belinda and Marty with Mrs. Towers and Riff, and ran toward the Soul, digging the keys from my pocket. Jamming them into the ignition, I shoved the gearshift into Drive and flew across the clearing to put distance between the burning barn and my car. Two Fairlawn Glen Safety Department patrol cars emerged from the dust storm.

I stumbled out of my car and stood staring at the burning barn, ignoring the bustling activity around me. A blaring siren penetrated my malaise. I turned with surprise as the big Glen fire truck lumbered into the clearing. A few minutes later small trucks spilled everywhere. My young friend, Thad, jumped from the cab of one. Hugging me to his chest, he shouted, "*Mrs. Barrett, are you all right?*"

I yelled into his face, "*Thad, what are you doing here?*"

"*Volunteer fireman,*" he explained.

"*How did you know about the fire?*"

"*Quinn called it in when he saw the smoke.*" With that he went running toward the fire truck.

Marty was cradling Riff and moved toward me along with Mrs. Towers and Belinda. I think that walker was the only thing holding them all up. Belinda didn't look so good. I may not know what concussed eyes look like, but hers weren't normal. Mrs. Towers looked a fright, but, pumped full of B12, that lady was amazing.

"Marty, there are two lawn chairs in the back of my car. Drag them over for Belinda and Mrs. Towers, please."

Passing Riff off to me, Marty went to work with the chairs, settling Belinda and then Mrs. Towers, who plopped heavily into the chair.

Cars were whooping everywhere. An ambulance bumped its way into the clearing, and I waved it toward us.

I babbled at the male paramedic at the back of the vehicle, "My friend Belinda fell and hit her head when—" I darted my eyes to meet Marty's—"when the fire broke out." I pointed at Belinda's foot. "She has to wear that idiotic balloon boot, and she stumbled and fell. You need to get her to the hospital." A female paramedic was poking and prodding both Belinda and Mrs. Towers.

Marty added, "You need to check out this old lady here."

Mrs. Towers threw him an angry look but ruined it with a fit of coughing.

The female paramedic yelled over her shoulder to her partner, "*Jay, get these people some oxygen and some water!*"

Mrs. Towers was shooing her away, croaking, "I'm fine. Take Belinda to the hospital."

Jay rushed over cradling several bottles of water and force-fed us some hits from an oxygen face mask. It was a surprisingly uplifting experience. "Whew," I mumbled, "no wonder Marcy sucks on that stuff." I removed the cupped gizmo and held it in front of Riff's snout.

The two paramedics fussed with us for a bit but eventually agreed that Belinda was the one in need of a ride to the hospital. They made quick work of securing her to a stretcher. I walked by her side, with Riff flopping in my arm like a limp fox wrap. I was reminded of escorting Mrs. Towers in a similar fashion at the garage rescue. I couldn't keep the tears from my voice as I consoled my best friend in the whole world, "Belinda, you're going to be all right. I'll meet up with you at the hospital."

Eyes closed, she squeezed my hand reassuringly. One, two, three, and they lifted her into the back of the ambulance. I laughed when Belinda growled, "Get that gawdawful boot off my foot!"

Thad and several other men were wrestling with the hoses beside the fire truck, and I recognized my friend Fireman Bob…whom Belinda and I know from our firehouse visits. I called over to him, *"Bob. Hey, Bob!"*

He stopped long enough to look over and holler, *"What?"*

*"You might as well let that barn burn. It's being torn down anyway! Just keep it contained so we don't end up with a forest fire!"*

Chief Braddock swung around the end of the fire truck and shouted, *"She's probably right, boys, but you guys do what you have to."*

Quinn met me halfway back to my car chuckling. "I knew it was just a matter of time until you joined the Safety Department." He caught me up in a hug and held me at arm's length. "You all right, Mrs. Barrett?"

I nodded and smiled up at him. "Yes, Chief, I'm all right."

"How did the fire start?"

I stammered, "Well, um… "

Overhearing the exchange, Marty stepped forward. "It was my fault, Chief Braddock. I lit a cigarette, and Mrs. Barrett started to give me hell, uh, heck about it, so I stubbed it out. Or at least I thought I did."

Quinn narrowed his eyes at Marty. "Who are you?"

"Marty Christmas."

Quinn's eyebrows shot up. "Well, Marty Christmas, how did you end up out here with these ladies?"

I groaned. "Quinn, can we save all this for later?"

With a brisk nod he ordered, "Come by my office in the morning and we'll talk. All right?"

"Sure, Quinn, all right." My chin wobbled.

Mrs. Towers yelled at him from her chair, *"Sheriff, don't you pick on Leslie or that boy! They saved us!"*

As though he was only just now noticing her, Quinn called, "Mrs.

Towers, we got a call from that nursing home in town about you."

She yelled, "*I'm not going back, Sheriff. You stay away from me!*"

Quinn threw a puzzled look my way. I grinned and shrugged an I-don't-know shrug.

He shrugged back, patted me on the shoulder, and moved off to see about whatever police people do in situations such as these. I settled into Belinda's vacant chair with a sigh. Marty's hair was sticking up on his head. His used-to-be-white t-shirt was now a dirty gray.

Mrs. Towers' face was streaked with ash, which hid the smears of brown eye shadow. She blew out a breath. "Boy, that was close."

"What?" I asked. "The fire? Or possibly getting hauled back to the nursing home?"

"The nursing home, of course. It takes more than a little-bitty fire to rattle me."

I grinned and turned to Marty. "There is a small bowl in the well of the front seat. Would you pour some of this water in it for Riff, please?"

Marty hopped to. "Sure, sure. Be glad to."

I suddenly remembered his old dog. "Hey, where's Rover?"

Marty sat on his haunches pouring water for Riff, who was already wriggling to get free. He's over there." Marty waved an arm toward a truck, where I saw a tumble of dogs resting on the ground. I recognized the big, solid lump as Rover and the two skinny, sticklike dogs as Cyd and Charisse. I realized Thad must have come straight from the junkyard when the call came in about the fire.

With Riff lapping and playing in the water, I looked at Marty. "Marty, see if Rover needs any water, then come back and tell us the rest of the story while we watch this old barn burn down."

Marty walked back with the bottle in his hand. He had poured some water into the palm of his hand. Rover slapped at it a couple of times, then dropped his head back onto the ground. Marty perched on the front-passenger seat, wiped his wet palm against his leg, and dangled his feet from the open car door.

"How old is Rover?" Mrs. Towers asked between gulps of water. She splashed some on her face.

He took a gulp of his own and replied, "About two hundred in dog years. My mother has been after me to let the vet put him down, but, well, you know, it's hard.

I looked at my own exhausted, face-dripping dog sitting on my foot and sighed. "Yeah…I can imagine."

"It isn't just about Rover. It has been hard: Grandpa dying, Mom working so much. She's scared we won't be able to manage without Grandpa's Social Security check, and then old Rover there." He shook his head and swiped at his eyes. "It's just been hard."

He looked at each of us in turn. "I'm sorry, you know, about scaring you with that shotgun. That's all I was trying to do, scare you. I thought maybe you knew what had happened to the money."

"What money?" I prompted, one-handing Riff to my lap.

Grandpa had a problem with liquor. He wasn't mean to us or anything. My mom was just glad he took us in when my dad ran off. Grandpa used to get drunk and tell me stories about the crazy things he did when he was young. Most of the stories would be twisted around every time he told them—you know, different endings and such—but one story never changed. He talked about a buddy by the name of Warren Keck. He said him and Warren used to break into people's houses to steal stuff and then drive to Knoxville and sell the stuff at pawn shops. In 1968—Grandpa was always consistent about the year and his buddy's name, Warren Keck. Anyway, he said that one night they broke into this really big house. They always went through the places quickly, usually concentrating on the master bedroom, looking for jewelry and whatnot. He said he was jamming watches and miscellaneous jewelry into his pocket when Warren whooped from the closet. Warren came running out with some kind of case. They laid the case on the bed and opened it. Grandpa said it was filled with coins all stacked up in little plastic sleeves. They figured they'd found a collection of old coins. Anyway, they took off for their truck. Grandpa tried to get Warren to split the coins with him, but Warren refused. He told Grandpa it was obviously a treasured collection, and they would get more for it if they sold it intact. When the two of them split up, Grandpa had the watches and stuff in his pockets, but Warren kept the box of coins. He told Grandpa he was going to lock it up in a locker at the terminal. Grandpa said Warren disappeared after that. He figured Warren had lit out with all the loot, and he was furious. He used to say over and over, 'None of us would be living in this broken-down old trailer, boy, if I had gotten my share of that money.'"

Once it was apparent that Marty was done talking, I nodded sagely. "They stole that collection from a numisma-whatsits. That's where the Kennedy half-dollar came from."

Marty and Mrs. Towers both responded with blank stares.

"A professional collector of old coins. I found an old coin wedged in the trunk."

"How come I didn't hear about this?" Mrs. Towers wheezed indignantly.

I waved her off. "I'll tell you about it later." I continued to Marty, "So, you heard about the body we found in the trunk of that old Rambler. What made you think it was Warren?"

"Thad Marshall bragged around town that he had gotten a look inside the trunk. He said he saw long strands of really black hair when the chief lifted the quilt. Grandpa always went on about how Keck had Elvis hair. He said the girls were all wild about that hair of his." He shrugged. "I figured it might be him."

"How did you know we were the ones who found the body?"

"Thad's grandpa and my grandpa were buddies. Since Grandpa died, Ray comes around once in a while to check on my mother and me. He likes to talk about how the two of you ladies—you and that Mrs. Honeycutt—solved the case of the turtle man out there at Lake Manchester. He laughed about how you talked Thad into prying open that trunk with his screwdriver."

Taking umbrage, I complained, "Obviously Thad blabs everything he knows to his granddaddy. It isn't like I manhandled him into using his screwdriver."

We flinched as loud *rat-a-tat* bursts sounded from the foggy barn. *BLOOEY... BLOOEY... BLOOEY BLOOEY BLOOEY.*

"Uh-oh," Marty mumbled. "The shells."

"Don't worry, Marty. The authorities aren't going to sift through everything like an arson squad. Who knows what the Madsens had stored in there? Could have been firecrackers or an old, discarded shotgun." I dismissed the explosions and reclaimed my seat. "You've already confessed to causing the fire. It was an accident."

Mrs. Towers huffed in agreement and sat back down. "Don't worry about it, Marty. We don't have any idea what caused those little explosions. She leaned forward to look around me at Marty. "How long have you been following Leslie and Belinda?"

"Just today. I parked in front of the townhomes and followed them into town. I saw them pull into the nursing home parking lot, so I drove back down the road a ways to wait for them to come out."

"You didn't know *I* was stowed away in the backseat!" she crowed.

Marty grinned. "No, ma'am, I didn't."

One of those uncensored nonsense observations I am known for burbled forth. "I wonder why the advertising people make M&M's into little people? When I see those commercials, I feel sorry for the

M&M people. It's a pretty warped, cannibalistic advertising campaign, if you ask me."

Nobody said a thing, but silence usually infers agreement. Fireman Bob wandered over and aimed a squinting question in my direction. "You people have any idea what was blowing up in there?"

Mrs. Towers was quick. "Bob, those Madsen people have been shoving crap into that old barn for a hundred years. Could have been old fireworks or something." She shrugged.

Bob narrowed his eyes, not at all convinced.

She waved him off. "Go back to your fire, Bob."

When Bob left to huddle with his firemen buddies, I grinned at my friend. "I'm impressed with your flimflam talent, Mrs. Towers." I took a swig from my water bottle. "Marty, what were you thinking? That we found stolen coins lying around Keck's remains and planned to sell them on the black market? Well, I did find that one half-dollar piece, but it was way under where we found the skeleton. But that's not the issue. I admit I did sweet-talk Thad and Tully into prying open that trunk, but what made you believe that we knew anything about those stolen coins?"

"Thad will tell anyone who will listen how the two of you are crackerjack detectives. I thought maybe you'd figured out where Warren had stashed the coins. That is, assuming the body in the trunk *was* the body of Warren Keck. I didn't know about that coin ya'll found."

"You and Belinda *are* good detectives, Leslie," Mrs. Towers seconded.

I nodded. "Well, even assuming that, there's no way we could have known about some cache of stolen old coins. It doesn't make any sense."

Marty blew out an exasperated breath. "I know. It was a dumb idea. I figured if you did know where the coins were, I could get my grandfather's half of the loot."

Mrs. Towers shrugged. "Those coins might not be worth squat."

He shook his head at her. "Grandpa said they were stacked in that case in little sleeves to protect them. He also mentioned some papers in there asserting to them being authentic."

"That Kennedy half-dollar is worth ten dollars today. Who knows what the value of the entire collection is now," I mused.

We were all quiet for several minutes as we watched the remaining roof of the barn fold in on itself. "Marty, you said your grandfather told you Warren was going to hide the loot in a locker at the terminal. What terminal?"

"I assumed he was talking about the Greyhound bus terminal in Clifton. That's the only terminal around here, but I went over there and poked around. You know, like I told the guy at the information desk that my grandfather just died, and he used to talk about storing personal stuff in one of their lockers. The man asked me what the number of the locker was, and of course I didn't know. Then he asked me for the combination to the lock. I told him my grandfather had stowed this personal stuff in a locker way back in the late sixties. That's when I learned that all the lockers in the bus terminal had been replaced with new ones back in the eighties."

"Maybe they found the loot when they opened an unclaimed locker," Mrs. Towers suggested.

"It's possible," I muttered. "Marty, do you know whether your grandfather ever worked on the railroad in Clifton?"

Marty scowled. "We don't have a railroad."

"There used to be. It closed in 1968, but the old Tennessee Central Railway depot is still there. Someone transformed it into a candy store."

"Oh, I've been in there," Mrs. Towers interjected. "That used to be part of a real railroad depot? That's fascinating."

I fiddled with Riff's collar. "So, I guess your grandfather never mentioned anything about a key?"

"What key?" Marty asked.

"What key?" Mrs. Towers echoed.

I told them both about the small key I had found on the quilt covering the body. "So far, all Belinda and I have figured out is that it belonged to a lock that had something to do with the Tennessee Central Railway. There are initials engraved on the rounded end, a *C*, then a worn off letter, an *R*, and another *R*, so we figure it stands for *Tennessee Central Railroad*. Oh, and there's the number forty-eight crudely engraved on the key. It could be the number of a locker."

Mrs. Towers beamed. "Oh my but you girls are good. Imagine the two of you ciphering out that clue! Amazing. I'm so proud of you."

"Mrs. Barrett, are you suggesting that Keck stashed the coins in a locker at the railroad terminal?"

I nodded. "It's possible. There are a lot of coincidences in this case. Keck and your grandfather stole the loot in 1968. Keck went missing, and now we know he died in 1968. The Tennessee Central Railway went out of business in 1968, and Elvis Presley's comeback TV special was in 1968."

Marty's head snapped up. "Elvis Presley? What does he have to do with all this?"

"Marty," I said, "Elvis Presley had something to do with everything."

# Chapter Eighteen

We stayed a bit longer, watching until the old barn was reduced to lumps of smoldering ashes.

Mrs. Towers wearily admitted, "Leslie, I'm fading fast. I need to go home and take a shower. I smell like burned toast and so do you."

"Yeah," I sighed. "I'll take you and Riff home and then run up to the hospital to check on Belinda. I forgot to send Belinda's purse along with her. They will need all her insurance stuff. If I don't move pretty soon, I'm afraid I won't be able to move at all."

We both creaked to our feet, and Marty started folding up the lawn chairs to stow in the back of the Soul. "What are you going to tell the police about me? About how I threatened you with a shotgun?"

Mrs. Towers looked at me aghast. "Leslie, do you remember being threatened with a shotgun?"

I returned her look. "Gee, it all happened so fast. It's all a blur."

"What about the fire? It was my fault."

"It was an accident, Marty. You probably did everybody a big favor burning down that old barn. It would have taken forever to knock it down."

The tension in his young face and shoulders sagged away. "Gosh, thanks. I know the gun was a dumb stunt. Honestly, I just wanted to make some money to help my mother and me out of a bad situation. What are you going to tell the chief about the coins, and the key, and the railroad?"

"Nothing yet. Quinn asked me to check in with him tomorrow morning. I was thinking about taking a trip over to that old depot slash candy store before I say anything to Quinn. Maybe I can get a lead on what happened to the old lockers. It's a long shot, Marty. Want to meet me there in the morning at ten o'clock?"

"Me too," Mrs. Towers insisted.

"We'll see how you're feeling in the morning. In fact, we'll see how *I* feel in the morning."

"I'll meet you at the candy store. I've got to go lug Rover into my truck, and that's no easy task."

Putting my hand on his arm, I said softly, "You need to let him go, Marty. You've got to love him enough to let him go."

"I know, Mrs. Barrett."

We watched him coax Rover over to his truck and laughed when he boosted the old dog into the cab. I waved at Thad, Fireman Bob, Quinn, and the rest of the crew as they sprayed water over the last of the burning debris.

Mrs. Towers wanted to (a) go to the hospital with me and check on Belinda or (b) go home. I refused both requests. "I would appreciate it if you would stay with me tonight, Mrs. Towers. You can have the guest room and bath. Watch Riff for me while I go and check on Belinda. You should call Valerie when you get to my place. The poor girl is probably a lunatic by now wondering what happened to you." She resisted both suggestions, but without her usual fervor.

Belinda wouldn't stay in the hospital overnight even though she did have a slight concussion, not to mention inhaling barn smoke. The hospital staff strapped her back into her balloon boot and loaded her into my car. On the way to my place I pulled into Food Stuff City. "I'm going inside to get a carton of those chocolate protein drinks, Belinda. Stay alert. The doctors said you need to stay awake."

"I know. I know. I'm a nurse, remember?"

I was only gone for ten minutes, but Belinda was fast asleep when I got back.

"Belinda." I jostled her arm.

"What?" She roused to my great relief. I drove with my left hand and shook her every few minutes with my right.

Slapping at my hand, she complained, "Leslie, leave *me* alone."

It went on like that for the fifteen minutes it took to pull into my garage.

On entering the house, I hollered for Mrs. Towers with no answer. I towed Belinda along with me, following the sound of my hair dryer into the master bathroom. Mrs. Towers had Riff standing on top of my vanity, her eyes closed, reveling in the low setting of the hair dryer. "We took a shower," Mrs. Towers explained. "I used your baby shampoo on Riff. I hope you don't mind me wearing one of your nightgowns. My clothes are tied up in a garbage bag in the garage. You girls need to wash off the stink of that old, burning barn." She wrinkled her nose with distaste.

Mrs. Towers babysat Belinda while I stripped, discarded my own smoky clothes in a garbage bag, and soaped up in the shower. It took both of us to de-frock and de-balloon Belinda. We squirted baby shampoo at her and put her under the shower spray long enough to rinse it off. That was the best we were going to be able to do tonight.

We wrapped Belinda in one of my hotel-style guest robes and propped her up in my bed with a chocolate protein drink. Belinda asked questions for a while, swooned, and then woke up again. With Belinda in my bed and Mrs. Towers in the guest bedroom, Riff and I crashed on the sofa. It was getting dark. It had been a crappy day. I monkeyed with my cell phone to set the alarm to go off every hour, intending to zombie-walk into the bedroom and jostle Belinda awake from her concussion coma. Evidently I did something wrong with the phone.

Realizing I had slept through the night without jostling Belinda back to life, it was a relief to hear her talking in the kitchen, making coffee. I ran my hand down the covers until I encountered Riff's warm, furry body. My hand caressed her tennis ball–sized head, and she licked my hand—which I hate—but I left my hand on her head and went back to sleep.

I was finishing another shower, still trying to get that smoky smell out of my hair when Belinda *yoo-woo*ed to tell me that Marty Christmas was on the phone. In a robe, and towel-drying my hair, I took the phone from Belinda's outstretched hand. "Marty? Uh-oh, what time is it?"

"Ten fifteen," he said, "I'm down at the candy depot."

Still a bit suspicious of young Marty, I asked, "How did you get my phone number?"

"I know where you live, Mrs. Barrett, remember? I was waiting in front of the townhomes yesterday for you and Mrs. Honeycutt."

"That doesn't explain how you got my phone number, Marty."

"Mrs. Barrett, you're in the phone book."

"Oh yeah, that makes sense. I'll meet you there in about forty-five minutes."

"Bring the key."

I hung up.

Even though she was still a bit foggy headed, Belinda insisted she was well enough to go along. Mrs. Towers didn't have the same investment in the key mystery as we did, so she opted to stay at my place with Riff. She had called her daughter the previous evening and let her know she was staying with me until we could make some minor modifications to her place. Valerie was upset with her, and with Belinda and me, for slipping away as we did, although she told her mother the doctor had called in her discharge order shortly after the staff realized she was missing. They told Valerie one of the dementia patients had wandered off, triggering the alarm. They didn't realize Mrs. Towers was gone until all the excitement was over.

Mrs. Towers was very diplomatic with her daughter. "Valerie, I'm perfectly fine. You know Leslie and Belinda. They wouldn't let anything bad happen to me." Of course, she said nothing about the incident out at the barn.

When we got to the depot, I was surprised the building was so small; the three of us piling in through the doorway felt like a crowd. An elderly lady slapped postcards onto a counter as though she were playing gin rummy. "Welcome to the Candy Depot," she said less than enthusiastically.

Belinda had insisted on going bootless, as she was expecting to soon escape from boot incarceration. I didn't argue, recalling my own booted days. I dragged Marty by the elbow and approached the counter. "Hello, my name is Leslie Barrett, and the limping lady behind us is my friend Belinda Honeycutt." I tugged Marty by his shirt. "And this young man is Marty Christmas. Isn't that the most unusual name you've ever heard? You know, Merry Christmas, Marty Christmas— such a cool name."

The lady favored Marty with a thin smile. "Yes, that's a very memorable name, young man."

Turning a higher-wattage smile my way, the lady asked, "May I help you look for anything in particular?"

"No, not really. Are you the owner of this quaint shop?"

Standing taller by about a half-inch, she replied, "Yes, as a matter of fact I am. My name is Ellen Usher. My husband and I own the shop. My father used to be an engineer with Tennessee Central Railway. It was a fine railroad back in its day. We jumped at the chance to display some of the railroad memorabilia here in the shop"—she lazily flung one arm outward—"as well as the refurbished railcar out front that sits on a preserved section of the actual tracks from the heyday of Tennessee Central."

I flicked my gaze about the shop. "And candy, you sell candy, don't you?"

Her head went up and down like a bobble head. "Yes, yes, of course. Please feel free to look around at our selection."

Belinda had been poking me in the ribs for the last few minutes and was beginning to annoy me. "What is it?" I whispered tersely over my shoulder.

Belinda's head appeared next to mine to whisper in my ear, "Leslie, look up and to your right. What do you see up there?"

I did as my friend suggested, and almost Snoopy-danced in place. A block of old lockers had been preserved with shelves built around them on both sides in a tasteful attempt at framing. Marty practically trampled me in his excitement, pounding around the counter toward the bank of lockers. He yelped, "Look, Mrs. Barrett."

Mrs. Usher hurriedly scolded, "Young man, you aren't supposed to be behind the counter."

Ignoring her, I followed Marty, and Belinda followed me. The three of us stood before the lockers as though they were a shrine to a long-forgotten island god. With a shaking finger I pointed. "Marty, look, forty-eight." The block of lockers was numbered forty-five through fifty, but forty-eight was the only one with a battered old lock.

From behind us Mrs. Usher asked, "Oh, are you history buffs of railroad paraphernalia?"

"Oh my, yes," I gushed. "Are these lockers from the old depot?"

The bobbling head bobbled. "I'm pleased you noticed them. My husband and I wanted to preserve parts of the old depot. We selected this bank of lockers because number forty-eight was the only locker that was still locked when the railroad closed down in 1968."

I frowned. "Why on earth haven't you opened it?"

"The fact that it remains locked to this day lends an air of mystery to it. We wanted to leave the contents to the visitors' imagination."

"But when the owner didn't return, wouldn't the railroad management have opened the locker? They must have had some type of protocol or time limit or something."

"From what my father told me, a man paid a deposit fee to keep the locker. Shortly after that the owners of the railway announced it was shutting down. It was all pretty sudden. Once word got out, people drifted in and collected their belongings, all except for number forty-eight. If the man's name was ever recorded, it's long since lost. Like I said, it became a mystery, and people made up romantic stories about why he never claimed the contents. The lock was still on the locker when my husband and I bought the place, so we decided not to disturb it."

In a solemn voice, and with my hand on Marty's shoulder, I said, "Mrs. Usher, young Marty's grandfather died recently. The only things he left behind for him was an old, dying dog and the key to locker number forty-eight at the old depot."

Her eyes grew to an enormous size. "What? But, but that can't be. Why on earth didn't his grandfather claim the contents of the locker after all these years?"

Marty's Adam's apple traveled up and down his throat convulsively. "My grandfather used to talk a lot about this locker. He always said he wanted me to have the contents when he passed on. He sort of built up the significance of the locker over the years. He had his reasons for not claiming the contents while he was alive."

Mrs. Usher began to stammer. "Well, I don't know about this. Is there some way you can prove it was your grandfather who reserved this locker forty-eight years ago?"

I met Mrs. Usher's eyes. "Is there some way you can prove he didn't? Why don't we try the key and see whether it fits?" I offered the key for her inspection. "See, Mrs. Usher, engraved on the key are the initials of the railroad, and the number forty-eight is scratched on it to identify the locker to which it belonged. If this key opens the lock, this pretty much proves that Marty's grandfather was the owner of the contents."

Belinda wheezed in my ear, "Leslie, are you sure we should?"

I flapped my hand at her to hush.

Mrs. Usher turned the key over in her hands and studied it almost reverently. "Yes, I see that. I don't know what to do. That locker has always been a source of mystery and conversation. Sort of romantic."

I shrugged. "There isn't any reason it can't remain a mystery and a source of conversation, Mrs. Usher. Why don't you allow young Marty here to insert the key? If it opens the lock, Marty can remove the contents while your back is turned. That way you can continue to tell customers—in all honesty—that the original owner never returned to claim the contents, whatever they are."

I grabbed the key from her hand before she had the chance to come up with any more objections. Going the legal route to gain access to that locker could take another forty-eight years. I handed the key to Marty. "Go ahead, Marty, see if the key fits."

"But...," Mrs. Usher sputtered.

"Go ahead, Marty," I ordered sharply.

Marty started at my tone and stabbed the small key into the lock. Holding the padlock firmly in his left hand he turned the key until the hasp opened with a reluctant *thwack*.

"Oh my goodness," Mrs. Usher exclaimed. "It fit, how remarkable. I think I'm going to cry."

"Turn around, Mrs. Usher," I urged the woman. "For the sake of future railroad aficionados, don't ruin the mystery of the locker."

Mrs. Usher turned her back. I'd bet she even closed her eyes as extra insurance. I nodded at Marty, and he eased the door open.

Belinda blurted excitedly, "Oh, Leslie, look…"

I did an elaborate pantomime of zipping my lips shut and caught Mrs. Usher's shoulders before she had the chance to turn around. "Yes, Belinda, I see. Marty, go ahead and remove the items. Your grandfather wanted you to have them."

There was a balled-up jacket stuffed into the locker and behind it what looked like an old cigar box. Marty pulled them out, wrapping the jacket around the box.

"Hand them to me, Marty, then close the locker and the lock. We don't want to ruin Mr. and Mrs. Usher's mystique about the unclaimed locker with its unknown contents. It's sort of like Al Capone's alleged vault. Geraldo Rivera ruined that mystery. We don't want to ruin this mystery."

"Can I turn around now?" Mrs. Usher sniffled.

"Give us a few minutes to leave, Mrs. Usher." I patted her shoulder.

Marty surprised me when he addressed Mrs. Usher's back, his voice quavering with emotion. "Thank you, ma'am, this means an awful lot to me."

Mrs. Usher emitted a soft sob. The three of us just about trampled one another getting out the door.

We hustled for a few steps, then stumbled to an abrupt stop at the sight of a Fairlawn Glen Public Safety patrol car sitting beside my Soul. Chief Quinn Braddock leaned against the driver's door with his arms folded. I cringed as Agent Hailey Donnelly climbed from the passenger seat.

Quinn looked over at us and ordered sternly, "Ladies, follow us to my office. It's time to clear the air and find out what you have been up to this time." He threw a finger in Marty's direction. "You too, young man." His gaze returned to me. "I recall asking you last night to come by my office this morning. When I called your house, Mrs. Towers answered and finally told me where you were, but she refused to tell me why you came to the Candy Depot."

I opened my mouth to make up something, but Belinda intervened. "We'll follow you to your office, Chief. I will not stand on the street and be harangued like a common criminal."

I was so proud.

Hailey hadn't said anything yet, but now she barked across the hood of the patrol car with a stabbing finger, "The two of you are a menace to society!"

I sucked in a furious breath in preparation for a tantrum. Belinda beat me to it, again. Stabbing her own finger at Hailey, she hollered, "None of this would have happened if you would just share information with law-abiding citizens when questions are asked of you!"

"*What?*"

"*That's enough, both of you,*" Quinn barked.

All traps immediately snapped shut, and he continued, "Meet us at my office." He gestured give-it-to-me with both hands. "Mrs. Barrett, give me whatever that is."

"What?"

Hailey smirked. "Don't get cute, Leslie."

"This jacket belongs to this young man here, Marty Christmas; it's just about the only thing he has left of his grandfather."

Quinn wiggled his fingers again. "C'mon, Leslie, hand it over."

I plopped the bundle into his arms. His eyes widened at the weight.

"Marty is going to want those back, Quinn." Putting a stop to the street show, I turned to Marty. "Marty, you can ride with us. We'll bring you back to your truck when we're done."

Marty nodded and climbed into the rear of my Soul. Hailey was yammering on about something, but I silently ignored her and slid behind the wheel of my car. As soon as Belinda's door slammed, Marty muttered, "Boy, this isn't looking good."

# Chapter Nineteen

Following Quinn's cruiser out of town, I said, "I vote we tell them everything."

Marty's breath caught, and I met his frightened eyes in the rearview mirror. "Marty, put on your seat belt." He scrambled to comply, and once he was safely clicked into place, I said, "We tell them everything, except for the part about Marty's shotgun fiasco."

"Leslie, you can't lie to the authorities. We already deceived Mrs. Usher back there."

I shook my head. "Belinda, you were married to a big-shot attorney from Philadelphia. We didn't lie to Mrs. Usher. We may have allowed her to come to some slightly bent conclusions, but we never told her an outright lie. Don't you ever watch those hearings on Capitol Hill?"

"There is a legal term for this, Leslie. It is called *obfuscation*. I'm concerned about the message we're sending Marty by not telling the whole truth."

"What does that mean?" Marty asked.

"It means what Leslie is telling us to do, Marty, is dance around to obscure the truth."

I glanced at my friend. "I am not responsible for young Marty's moral edification. I'm just trying to keep the kid out of jail."

"Thank you, Mrs. Barrett," Marty piped up from the backseat.

"You're welcome. Oh, and, Marty, why aren't you in school?"

"Um...well."

"Marty, I'll make you a deal. You go back to school and graduate, and I won't blab your shotgun exploits to the cops. Do we have a deal?"

"Deal. So, what are we going to say was the reason I was in the barn?"

We agreed on the real story about Marty's grandfather, and Warren Keck. Elaborating about shotgun shells was felt to be incidental. I told Belinda to keep her moral conflicts to herself.

We piled out of the car and followed Quinn and Hailey into the Safety Department and into Quinn's little conference room, the only room with an actual door. Officer Mark Edwards followed us in and greeted us with a smile.

Hailey was carrying the jacketed bundle and placed it on the table. We stood and watched as she folded back the jacket and flipped up the lid on the box. Belinda, Marty, and I did everything but climb on top of the table to get a look inside.

"The three of you need to sit down," she almost shouted. "This is police business."

"Oh, shut-up, Hailey," I snapped irritably. We continued to stare over Hailey's shoulders at the open box on the table.

Marty blew out a "Wow, it's just like Al Capone's vault."

"Al Capone's vault was empty, Marty, except for a few old, empty bottles. It amounted to a lot of hype over nothing." Hailey spun around to fix me with a glare. I muttered, "You really need to get over yourself, Hailey," and proceeded to take a seat at the conference table.

A chuckle escaped Mark before he could rein it in. When everyone was settled at the table, I inquired, "Aren't you going to offer us some coffee or something?"

Quinn tossed a furious frown my way but said to Mark, "Would you mind getting a pitcher of water and some glasses for our *guests*?"

"No problem, Chief." Mark left the room quietly, but I heard a guffaw after the door shut behind him.

"Start at the beginning, ladies," Quinn ordered, tapping his pen against a pad of paper.

"Where we came into the story, or do you want us to back up to the real beginning? The one where Warren Keck ended up on the floor of the old Madsen barn with a broken neck and got himself dumped into the trunk of that old Rambler by Denver and Marcy Madsen?"

Hailey's mouth dropped open, and Quinn's eyes widened in surprise. Mark knocked on the door, and Marty hopped up to open it. As Mark was lowering the tray onto the table, Hailey fumbled to form words. "How did you know about Warren Keck?"

Mark chased his eyes around the table. "Uh-oh. What did I miss?"

"Take a seat, Mark." I smiled. "This is what happened. Once it was clear that Hailey was not going to share any information about the man in the trunk, we…" I proceeded to lead them through our Internet search for missing persons. None of them were familiar with Gus Tubman's disappearance in 1971.

Scooting forward in my chair I asked excitedly, "Did any of you ever see Elvis Presley's 1968 TV special? Don't you find it curious that after that Elvis allegedly went off to Vegas, got fat, and died?"

Belinda's warning voice stopped me. "Leslie, don't go there."

With a nod, I acquiesced. "Yeah, okay, never mind, it's just a theory of mine. Okay, so…"

"Tell them about the key, Leslie." Belinda beamed proudly. "I researched the key and connected it to the Tennessee Central Railway."

I pawed through my purse and produced the key. Hailey reached for it, but I drew it back and made a big deal out of presenting it to Quinn. He turned the key over in his hand, squinted at the engraving, then handed it to Hailey.

I told them all of it: how Thad Marshall had mentioned that his grandfather grew up with Denver Madsen, and our visit with Ray

Turner, which led us to Marcy Scrimger at the assisted living wing of the nursing home. I detailed Marcy's account of the circumstances surrounding Keck's launch from the hayloft at the hands of Marcy's brother, Denver, and the subsequent stuffing of Warren into the trunk of the Rambler. How Denver tossed the Rambler's keys down an old well, and… "Well, that was that, until the day Thad dragged the Rambler from the barn and jimmied the lock open."

Belinda opened her purse and produced our two evidence Baggies. "Here is the evidence Leslie collected from the trunk of the Rambler."

Hailey bristled. "When…?"

"Calm down, Hailey," she admonished. "Your people had the Rambler towed out to Marshall's when you were through examining it. Leslie wasn't satisfied that all the forensic evidence had been gathered. As it turned out, she was correct." She slid the Baggies over to Quinn, who slid them over to Hailey. "Marcy told us the only person who ever came looking for Warren was another fella about the same age. We know now that the fella was Marty's grandfather. Oh, and Denver dumped Warren's car somewhere. The license plate and keys went down the well with the keys to the Rambler."

Marty picked up the story from there. "My father took off when I was born, and my mother and I stayed with his father. My grandfather was an alcoholic and told a lot of stories about all the trouble he used to get into when he was a young kid. One story was always consistent."

Marty led them through his grandfather's retelling of his grandfather and Warren's breaking, entering, and stealing exploits, ending with their last job and Warren's discovery of the box of old coins in a closet. "All grandpa knew was what Warren told him; that is, Warren said he was going to lock up the box of coins in a locker at the terminal. Their plan was to let the fuss over the stolen coins die down, reclaim the box from the locker, and take the coins to Knoxville to see what they could get for them. Warren disappeared, and Grandpa figured he had run off with the coins, leaving Grandpa high and dry. Of course, now we know that Warren took a high dive from the hayloft."

Mark jumped in. "Where did you find the key?"

"I found it," I admitted, "when Thad opened that trunk. I looked around inside and settled on that bony hand. Then I noticed a glint of something on top of the quilt, and I picked it up without giving it much thought. I stuck it in my pocket and forgot all about it, for a while."

"You should have immediately turned over that key," Hailey harped in her I'm-with-the-TBI harpy voice.

"I *told* you, Hailey. I *forgot* about it for a *while*. Belinda and I have been cooped up for weeks because of her stupid foot. When you wouldn't tell me anything, we decided to do a little behind-the-scenes snooping of our own. If that is against the TBI law, then you can just slap on the cuffs right now." I dangled my wrists a few inches above the tabletop.

Mark snorted another laugh, Quinn threw him a glare, and Marty resumed his story. "My grandfather and Thad Marshall's grandfather were old buddies. Ray Turner checks in with my mother and me from time to time, and he likes to talk about how Mrs. Barrett and Mrs. Honeycutt tracked down that Abner fella's killers. When Mr. Turner told us about the body in the trunk, and that the body had long, black hair..."

Quinn whiffed his hand across the tabletop. "Wait a minute, what?"

"My grandfather had told me that Warren Keck had long, black hair. He said all the girls got all moony over him because he had Elvis hair. Anyway, Thad got a look inside the trunk and saw the long, black hair. When I heard that, I figured the man in the trunk might be Warren Keck."

Marty nervously looked at me. I continued the story "Marty knew where Belinda and I lived from Ray Turner's stories, so Marty followed us to the nursing home when we went to collect Mrs. Towers, and then on to the barn."

Quinn's eyes narrowed, so I gushed, "The three of us, well, plus Riff and Marty's two-hundred-year-old hound dog, Rover, were standing in the barn discussing everything. Marty mashed out his cigarette at my insistence, and shortly after that Mrs. Towers toddled in from the car. Suddenly, there was this big *WHOOSH* of flames, and the barn went up like, well, like an old, dried-out barn filled with old, dried-out hay. I clawed my way through the smoke with Riff and Mrs. Towers while Marty rescued Belinda and his dog." I shook my head and offered an old lady cough. "It was a *horrifying* experience."

I looked at Hailey's and Quinn's skeptical faces and then over at Mark, who was grinning like a fool. "Could have happened that way, I guess," Mark offered.

"I don't believe most of this story." Hailey snorted.

"Tough, Hailey," I said crossly. "You should seek help for your conspiracy problem."

Once again Mark came to the rescue. "Well, I for one am impressed at the way you and Mrs. Honeycutt unraveled the story behind the man in the trunk. You even figured out that the key was to a locker at the old railroad depot."

I nodded and wound up with the story about the preserved locker at the Candy Depot and its ongoing mysterious appeal.

Quinn looked at Belinda and me in turn and smiled. "So, the three of you conned Mrs. Usher into letting you open the locker and remove the contents?"

I opened my mouth to complete the spin, but Belinda beat me to it. "We told her that Marty's grandfather had died, and that the contents now belonged to Marty, which isn't legally untrue. Mrs. Usher didn't object and chose not to watch as Marty opened the locker and removed the contents."

I bobbled my head. "That's true, and this way, Mrs. Usher can continue to spout the mystery of the locker and its contents."

"Well, we're going to have to clear that up with Mrs. Usher," Quinn said solemnly.

"That's your call, Chief. You know, it's just possible the Ushers will get more mileage out of the real story than they would perpetuating the locker mystery," I suggested.

Nobody said anything for a while, so I poured myself a glass of water. Following a few sips, I asked, "Hailey, how did you learn the identity of the man in the trunk?"

"His wallet was in his pocket. Driver's license and everything," Hailey replied softly.

I shook my head sadly. "See, Hailey. You could have avoided this whole mess by just giving me the name of the guy in the trunk."

She smirked. "Oh, come on now, Leslie. Don't pretend you would have been satisfied with his name."

I raised my chin and turned to Quinn. "Is that all, Quinn? You have the whole story, the coins, and with a little digging through police records in this area, you can probably even figure out which numis-ta-whatsit the coin collection belonged to."

"Numis…what?"

"Numismatics: the study and collecting of old coins," Marty proudly informed him.

Hailey's tone was crammed with sarcasm. "And I have no doubt you fully intended to turn over the coin collection."

Belinda huffed. "Just what are you suggesting, Agent Donnelly? Are you attempting to slander our reputations?"

Belinda was really coming through. She had picked up a lot from her drunken attorney husband. At least he had been good for something.

"Come on, Leslie. We're done here." Stabbing Hailey with narrowed eyes, Belinda almost growled, "Unless you intend to charge us with something, which would be ridiculous. We need to get young Marty here back to his truck, and we need to get home and check on Mrs. Towers. She just got out of a nursing home, you know. We all almost lost our lives in an inferno yesterday afternoon, and not only that, but my foot hurts."

The three of us stood and walked to the door. No one stopped us from leaving, but I could hear Hailey's complaining, whiney voice through the closed door, and Mark's whooping laughter.

That guy is a hoot.

# EPILOGUE

Forty-eight years ago, in 1968, Buford Connors, a numismatist, had been the proud owner of an excellent collection of rare coins until two twenty-three-year-old punks broke into his house and made off with thirty years' worth of collecting.

Although Mr. Connors did not have his collection under lock and key, he had had the foresight to insure his collection for twenty-five thousand dollars and had long ago collected the full policy value from the insurance company. The company offered to pay a recovery fee of five thousand dollars for the collection's return. Belinda, Mrs. Towers, and I want the payout to go to Marty Christmas. Without the information Marty had shared concerning his grandfather and Warren Keck's shenanigans, the coins would have never been found. Marty thinks that Belinda and I should collect the reward; however, Belinda and I were chasing the mystery of a corpse and a key, not a collection of rare coins.

Thad offered Marty a job when school lets out for the summer. Until then Marty helps out around the junkyard after school. According to Ray Turner, Cyd and Charisse keep the young man company during his chores. Marty still feels the loss of Rover but has taken to the graceful, dancing greyhounds. If Marty is the recipient of the reward money as we expect, his mother is looking into some technical training so she can make a career change from waitressing to "pretty much anything else." Then they can look into more comfortable living arrangements.

Mrs. Usher doesn't hold any grudges since there has been renewed interest in the Clifton Candy Depot. Once the story started making the rounds in the papers and around town, people started swarming the place. The Chamber of Commerce is even setting up a website to promote the depot in the hope it will generate some tourism. Apparently, there are thousands of people fascinated with old railroad stuff. Who knew?

Belinda was medically released from boot incarceration the day following our powwow with Chief Braddock and Agent Donnelly at the Safety Department. Mrs. Towers is close to being back to her old self, with some concessions on her part. Her hairdo trips into Clifton have been slashed to once a week, and Belinda and I take turns driving her back and forth. She also faithfully carries her help-gizmo in the pocket holster she keeps strapped to the walker. She's taken to calling the gizmo Trigger.

All in all, things worked out pretty well for everyone, except Warren Keck. Agent Hailey Donnelly made some noise about potentially charging Marcy Scrimger with some kind of forty-eight-year-old crime. Belinda masterfully pointed out that the TBI may not want to prosecute Marcy. The visual of a frail, wheezing, oxygen-hugging, COPD-ridden old lady all over the papers would not be good press for the TBI. So nothing ever came of that. Nobody even cared that Marty had burned down the old barn, accidentally.

Two weeks after we revealed all to Quinn and Hailey, Belinda, Riff, and I were helping Mrs. Towers stack her knickknacks and snow globes on some shelving units that now line the walls of her living room. Sitting in a recliner with Riff's butt planted on her foot, Mrs. Towers called out, "So, girls, what are we going to tackle next? Now that all the excitement has died down, I'm starting to get antsy."

I strained to balance a Niagara Falls snow globe on the highest shelf only to have Belinda snatch it from my grasp and settle it in place. "Well, the young Italian widow moved into Abner's place last week. I hear she's having an open house. I'm going to that one. And I'm still fascinated by Gus Tubman's disappearance back in 1971," I offered.

Mrs. Towers one-handed Riff into her lap. "Who is, or was, Gus Tubman?"

"Leslie." Belinda sighed. "You aren't going to start all that again, are you? The next thing I know you'll be snooping around Graceland looking for Elvis in a shallow grave."

"Elvis!" Mrs. Towers all but squealed. "Did you girls ever see his comeback special in 1968? Lordy but that boy looked good. I'm pretty sure I have it on a tape around here somewhere. I ordered it special."

Left hand held high, I brandished my yellow Swiffer in the attack stance made famous by Zorro. With a poke to her chest, I growled, "Okay, old lady, hand it over."

Hello Readers,

I can't see or hear you but if you're reading this, then you've just read my book, *Rambler*.

Thanks for allowing Leslie & Belinda to inhabit your brain for a bit. They run around in mine like a couple of caffeinated hamsters.

A brief review of your reading experience on Amazon, Goodreads, or another review site that I haven't discovered yet would be greatly appreciated. I want my publisher to keep signing up my books, but I need something to point to when I say "Well, someone liked them!" And be sure and check out the first two books in the Leslie and Belinda series, *Daredevil* and *Shanghaied*.

Follow me on Facebook, and check out my website to keep track of what I'm up to. By the way, it seems that Leslie & Belinda have already caught the scent of another mystery in the Glen and I can't wait to release the hamsters!

~ *Linda*

Follow me on:
Facebook: Linda S. Browning
Twitter: @LindaSBrowning
Website: lindabrowning.net